Table of Contents

Billionaire's Pleasure

The French Billionaire
Billionaire Romance

The Fallen Revenge
Billionaire Romance

The Fallen Revenge 2
Billionaire Romance

Billionaire's Pleasure

By: Dark Mocco

☐ **Copyright 2015 All rights reserved.**

In no way is it legal to reproduce, duplicate, or transmit any part of this document in either electronic means or in printed format. Recording of this publication is strictly prohibited and any storage of this document is not allowed unless with written permission from the publisher. All rights reserved.

Respective authors own all copyrights not held by the publisher.

Chapter One

Allen couldn't help but to sigh a little as he made his way to the penthouse. He knew that traveling was something he usually enjoyed, but today he just wasn't feeling it. He didn't care that there were men and women already falling at his feet or that the view was fantastic as always. All he could do was sigh. He was tired of the same old routine, and he was hungry.

I'll have to go hunting tonight. He thought to himself, but even that seemed unappealing. He sighed to himself before he caught sight of the girl that was walking beside him. Emily was none the wiser as Allen started to look at her. His eyes drifted to see what she was doing as he took in her form. She was apologizing to a guest down the hall, and yet for some reason Allen found her stunning.

He couldn't help but to grin to himself, shaking his head as if to ignore the fact that everything about her seemed to sing to him. Her very blood made his fangs want to come out and pierce her flesh as he made her moan underneath him.

Allen had to force himself to shake away the thoughts. He sighed a little as he leaned against the door, watching her. Many men would pretend to be having trouble with their keycard, but he felt no shame staring at her. His gaze refused to waiver as he took in every inch of her curvy form.

She had curves that seemed to delight him. Her ample breasts and hips were enough to make him want to take her in his arms, and suddenly for Allen hunting seemed to be one of the best things he could think to do, but with the sun still up it wasn't time. *Not even in these hallways.* He mused. Allen did hate being on a day schedule, but when caring for his fortune business calls could not be made during the night.

Much to his dismay. He sighed as she looked at him, and he caught her amber gaze. He winked at her, and for just a moment Emily felt her heart stop in a way. There was something about the man that made her stutter over her words before she apologized one more time.

He decided that he had stared long enough, and her uniform told him that she certainly did work at the hotel. It was all the information he needed. *I'll find you later.* He thought, as his gaze met hers one more time. She blushed, and soon enough she started to walk away as he disappeared into his room.

"It's not too bad." Allen ended up saying to himself. The colors weren't to his liking, but green would just have to do.

At least it's forest. He thought. The last thing he wanted was some neon or lime green to be dealing with. His hands raked over the sheets, seeming semi satisfied with the quality, and he couldn't help but to chuckle to himself thinking that whoever he did end up taking back would most likely think of them as luxurious. *If only they knew.* His house was full of so much more luxury than this, and it was something that he quite enjoyed.

Allen looked around the room until his eyes landed on his cooler and he put in the passcode. After the last incident of someone sneaking in to see what he was doing, he didn't want to deal with anyone else finding out about the contents of it. With a click, Allen reached in to find the blood bag. He sighed to himself contently right before his fangs pierced the sleek plastic, drinking deeply.

It took him only a moment to drink the bag dry, and he felt sated for a little while longer. He smiled to himself as he looked around, checking his accounts on his phone. His mind was far from business, though. All he could think about was hunting and finding out about the amber eyed girl that he had just seen. He smiled a little, and he started to lock the ice chest again, knowing that it would be a disaster if someone had seen.

For now, he started to lay down on the bed after putting his phone on loud to wake him up, knowing that after so much exposure to the sun he should sleep. Trying to get comfortable on the sheets, he couldn't seem to. Despite his tiredness he was restless in a way that he had yet to be in a while. So instead, Allen ran his fingers through his hair one more time before going to the shower, which he was pleased to see could be steam or jet.

He started to unbutton his dark black silk shirt, and slowly it slipped to the floor exposing his toned, pale chest. He could distinctly remember the last girl running her fingers over the smooth, marble like surface before he helped her up from her knees so that he could bite into her. It had been too long since he had more than a blood bag, and he chuckled, finally stepping into the shower and putting the water on high.

The jets massaged his aching muscles, but every time he closed his eyes he could see the girl and his cock twitched at the thought of having her under him. His hand traveled to wrap around it, but he stopped himself. *I'm better than that.* He said with nearly a growl, and that's when he decided that he'd have her. No matter what.

Chapter Two

Emily could kick herself. All she wanted to do was go home, and yet she had been talked into an extended shift. *I need the money.* She thought as she sighed, but it didn't make it any better. She couldn't help but to shake her head as she gritted her teeth. She just didn't like that they were bouncing her from station to station.

Working the desk would be one thing, but food service? She tried not to scoff, but it's what she hoped she'd avoid by working for a hotel in the first place. *To no luck.* She sighed. With that, she put on the apron, washing up just the way she needed so that she could go up. *Room 1021.* She thought to herself, sighing as she started to wheel the cart into the elevator, hoping that she would get lucky and no one would pop in to ride with her.

The last thing she needed was someone contaminating the food cart. She was happy to see that she went up there without any hassle at all, and the one person that did actually start to get in stopped at the look on her face. She couldn't help but to smile as she started to go to the room, checking the numbers as she went. She smiled as she knocked loudly, waiting.

It was a minute before anyone answered, and she wanted to sigh a little more as Emily knocked harder. She hated to be kept waiting. Just as Emily was going to knock a third time the door opened, and there was a very hot, angry looking man staring at her with just a towel wrapped around his waist. She could see his dark, curly happy trail that hinted at what was beneath that towel, and he smirked a little as she looked at him completely unsure of what she should say.

"Did you come here to deliver the food or to gawk at my body?" The man smirked a little as he looked at her. She couldn't help but to blush deeply, and she feared that it would be creeping down her neck soon enough. His eyes seemed to look right through her. She started to push the cart in, eager to leave as the man closed the door before him.

"Your order…" She said, seeming to stumble over it, trailing off in the end.

"Yes, I believe it would be unless you have the wrong room." He continued to tease her, and her blush did start to creep down her neck and to the top of her breasts. She only wished she had the buttons done up a little more.

"I assure you that it's fine, sir." She said, trying not to sound tight. Emily reminded herself that it was important that she be polite.

He was obviously a paying customer who had more than enough money by the suite that he had chosen, but there was something about his tone that already had her getting defensive.

"You assure me, huh?" He teased her, closing the door a little, and something in her heart pounded as Allen stepped in the way of the door.

"Are you new at this?" He purred a little bit, and she couldn't believe that she thought he was purring. She couldn't help but to blush, and Emily immediately shifted her attention so that she could work on everything else that was going on. She lifted the tray, starting to set everything up for him.

"Would you like me to leave the cart or put it on the table?" She asked, and her voice barely came above a whisper.

"You can just leave it there." He said, and with that he stepped out of the way just enough for her to squeeze by, but something about him captured her in his gaze. She shook herself out of it as she bowed her head and walked out. Allen watched her go, and he couldn't help but to grin a little bit. *Emily.* He thought, having read her nametag. *That name will just have to do.* He opened the door.

"Oh, Emily." He called down the hall, making her freeze and turn around. He watched as she put on a smile to make it seem as if she wasn't both aroused and freaked out.

"Yeah?" She said as casually as possible.

"I'd like some wine in an hour." He said.

"I get off in an hour." Emily blurted out, and she immediately regretted it. For some reason his smirk just widened a little bit.

"Oh? I'll call your manager and see." He said, and with that he shut the door. Emily was steaming as she made her way down to the main floor, and she couldn't wait to clock out. Little did she know that Allen really was calling her manager who was standing there with a sour expression on his face.

"You pissed him off." Mr. Roberts said, and she looked at him, nearly gaping.

"Pissed him off?" She exclaimed, and yet he shook his head.

"Look, Mr. Deval is a very important man here, and it's important he's happy. You're going to bring that wine and apologize. I will pay you for the time, but if you aren't there you're fired." He huffed before he walked away, and she was left there staring as the time passed by slowly.

Luckily, she was put on desk duty, and so the hour ticked by without Emily having to deal with anyone else, but it also left her completely to her thoughts. She couldn't ignore the pounding in her heart, and every time she thought about the strange, insistent man, she could feel herself blushing as she thought about him with only that towel wrapped around his waist. Her boss gave her a look as he held up the bottle of wine and cart an hour later, and she gritted her teeth as she put on a fake smile, going to the elevator once more. She had no idea what to expect.

Chapter Three

Allen waited, making sure that his shirt was mostly buttoned up, but he left two buttons undone. He couldn't help but to smile a little as he tapped his foot, looking at the empty trays. He did always enjoy this hotel. *They have great food.* He thought. He tapped his foot, smiling as he heard the knock, and he reveled in making her wait. He knew she was thinking about him with a towel on, and he couldn't wait to see her expression with him cleaned up. He opened the door, letting her in without a word. Emily's eyes raked over him, and she blushed a little bit.

"Your wine." She said, and he kicked the door closed gently, making sure it didn't slam. Emily looked at him confused as her heart started to pound.

"I'm sorry I made you nervous. I'm so cranky after a long ride." He said, and she looked him in the eyes. *That's right.* He thought, and for a moment she was caught in that gaze, swearing she could see a flash of red. She felt her body relax, and she smiled a little.

"It's fine." She said, feeling a little better with the man.

"You're off work now. I just wanted the manager to send you up." He said, smiling a little, and she nodded. *It seems reasonable.* She thought, but something nagged at her.

"I'm sorry." He said, popping open the wine bottle which came with two glasses in case he had a guess. He poured into both, smiling as he put them down for a minute.

"I realized I've yet to introduce myself." He said. "Allen Deval. It's a pleasure to meet you Emily." He said, putting the wine glass in her hand as she stared at him, seeming almost lost. She took it, and Emily took a sip, unsure what to say.

"A pleasure to meet you as well." She said before taking another sip, and his smile grew. He lounged in the chair in the sitting room, motioning for her to sit as well. Emily thought for a moment, but when glancing into his eyes she found herself sitting down.

"See. You're relaxing." He said, chuckling deeply, and she couldn't help but to get wet even though she tried to hide it. There was something about those eyes and that deep chuckle that pulled her in, but out of the corner of her eye she could swear that there was a flash of red.

"I suppose so, but I should really get going." She said, and he shook his head still smiling lightly.

"Why is that? You can enjoy yourself after work." He said teasing her, and she blushed a little.

"I suppose so." She replied, and Allen just shook his head.

"Wait. Am I keeping you from someone?" He said, and he tipped the wine to pour her another glass as she finished her first. His hand brushed her arm, making her shiver. She looked at him, and he was still standing close as her hands shook while she took another drink.

"No." She squeaked out, and he shook his head almost in disbelief.

"I can't believe that. A beautiful girl like you? There must be someone waiting at home." He said, as if daring her to tell him otherwise, and she shook her head. Emily had lost her voice with those eyes staring at her.

"Beautiful?" She said, and she put her wine glass down. He smiled, and Allen didn't take another moment before he put two fingers under her chin, gently tilting it up to look her in the eyes.

"Gorgeous." He whispered before his lips met hers.

It was fire in her veins as he kissed her, and she could feel her pussy growing wetter by the moment as his lips moved over hers in a dance she wasn't expecting. She couldn't help but to groan as her eyes fluttered closed and his fingers wrapped in her hair. She shivered when Allen pushed his tongue over hers, caressing it as if he knew exactly how to play her where she was moaning with parted lips when he finally broke it and pulled away.

He smiled at her, tracing a finger down her cheek and to her neck. Allen traced the curve of her vein as she groaned a little, looking over him. Emily's eyes raked down, and she could see the bulge in his pants. It was large, and her eyes widened. A soft moan escaped her lips again as he chuckled, and Allen leaned down to whisper in hear ear. His breath was hot against her, and it made a shiver run down her spine.

"I know you're wet." He teased her, and she started to bite her bottom lip, unable to respond.

She just looked up at him where he kissed her one more time. Allen pressed his lips to hers a little more aggressively this time as his hands went around the back to unsnap her bra. He pulled her top off of her, and Emily let him as she blushed. Her bra slid to the ground, and she was left in just her skirt and the small heels she was wearing. Allen's fingers reached down to tweak her nipple, rolling it between his fingers as she groaned.

"You want this don't you?" He asked her, knowing he wanted to hear her say it. He tugged on her nipple a little harder when all she did was moan, and her attention snapped back to him.

"Yes." She whispered after he repeated the question, arching into his hands as he started to tweak and tug on her other nipple, sending shivers of excitement through her.

She could feel her wetness starting to make a damp spot on her silky panties, and little did she know that Allen could smell it. He groaned as the smell of her blood and arousal mingled together, setting everything about him on edge. She closed her legs together tightly, but he smirked as he kissed her neck, wanting to sink his fangs into her. *Just not yet.* He reminded himself as her shaking fingers went to undo his shirt.

Chapter Four

"Then get on your knees." He whispered, and she could feel her heart hammering in her chest, but she looked up at him unable to move.

Allen repeated the statement, and Emily couldn't help but to gulp. She slowly got up to sink to her knees, balancing precariously on her heels, trying not to tip over. She bit her bottom lip, looking up at Allen, but she already knew what he wanted. Her shaking, excited hands went to reach up so that she could start to unbutton his pants, pulling the zipper down and soon freeing his hard, pre-come dripping cock.

Allen smiled down at her, and for a moment she could have sworn that she saw a flash of fangs, but she tried to put that behind her. Emily reminded herself that it was impossible, but her heart was pounding in her ears as she wrapped her delicate hand around the throbbing hard cock, stroking it gently as Allen tsked above her. She leaned in to kiss and lick on the head, gathering the pre-come up on her tongue before swallowing the already salty liquid.

Emily's eyes fluttered closed, and she moaned a little as that damp spot on her panties only grew. Her hand traveled between her legs, pulling her skirt up and sliding under her panties so she could stroke a finger up and down her wet, dripping slit. Allen smirked as his fingers wrapped up in her hair, making her moan again. He made sure to smear the pre-come from the tip of his cock over her lips before she opened her mouth to wrap her lips around the head.

She started to suck lightly as she swirled her tongue around the bottom. Her own finger started to stroke her clit, rubbing it in small circles as she moaned around the tip. Her hand still firmly held the base of Allen's cock, and she could feel it twitch as she moaned. He groaned above her, and Allen tightened his grip in her hair as he tried to keep from bucking into her mouth. He could feel her as she started to take a little more of his cock into her mouth, and he could see Emily's cheeks start to stretch as his cock started to disappear into her mouth.

She started to rub her clit, pinching it lightly as he started to force her to take more of it into her mouth. She couldn't help but to moan a little more as his cock hit the back of her throat, making her gag a little. She started to slide her fingers down her slit, opening her folds as she started to slide two fingers deep inside of her twitching pussy. She groaned a little more, and Allen started to fuck into her mouth, making her deep throat him.

She gagged a little more, gasping when he pulled back to where just the tip of his cock was at her lips, and she looked up to meet his gaze. For a moment, she saw a flash of red, but she was already lost in the touch of the strong man and his cock which throbbed in front of her lips. She started to bob up and down on it all on her own, and her free hand went to start to stroke his balls. Her fingers played over the skin delicately, and Allen groaned again.

"God." He groaned, and Allen didn't have anything else to say.

All he wanted to do was fuck her throat, but he knew that he wanted her to enjoy it to, and so he had to wait. He could see that her fingers were busy fucking in and out of her own pussy, and he wanted to be plowing into her. *Soon enough.* He thought to himself before she started to suck on him all over again, forcing his thoughts away from anything besides her hand that was rubbing his balls, massaging them, and her throat which was starting to spasm around his cock head every time she took him all the way in.

He started to pull her up and down by her hair, and her fingers were working furiously in and out of her pussy as her thumb reached up to continue to rub her clit, slowly teasing it. She could feel herself starting to build to orgasm, and Allen could tell as well. His own cock was starting to throb, feeling himself getting closer to his own orgasm, but Allen had no intention of coming in her mouth.

She started to explode in orgasm, clenching around her fingers as her thumb slowed down when rubbing her clit. He could feel her moans vibrating up his cock as he held her on his cock with her lips wrapped around the base, throat spasming around him before he pulled out. He pulled her off carefully by her hair as she moaned and gasped for air. She looked up at him, lips parted as she panted. Allen could still smell her arousal, but now it seemed to fill the entire air.

All he wanted to do was to take her, but she was still balancing on her heels with her skirt riding up around her hips and hand in her panties. He smiled as he pulled her up, and Emily stumbled into his chest. He nipped at her neck, fangs grazing. He knew that Emily felt it, but she was beyond caring or suspecting anything at all. All Emily could do was moan as her hand slid out of her panties, and Allen reached around to unzip her skirt, letting it slide down her legs.

He helped her to step out of it before he started to slide her wet panties down as well. They were around her ankles, and Allen stepped back to take in the view. He looked at her perky nipples, her breasts jiggling with each and every breast, to her curvy hips and exposed pussy. His eyes raked down, and he could see those wet panties around her high heel clad ankles, and he couldn't help that his cock throbbed all over again.

Chapter Five

Allen smiled as she stepped out of her panties, leaving them on the floor as well. He smiled as he pulled her to the bed. He couldn't help but to smile, leading her to sit on the bed as he flipped their positions. He kissed her neck again, kissing down to her breasts as his cock throbbed, but Allen choose to ignore his own climbing orgasm for now. All he wanted to do was kiss between her breasts before going to one nipple. He let his teeth graze over it, nearly piercing it, and she as lost in the pleasure as pain trickled in to mix with it.

He sucked on it gently, flicking his tongue over it before going to the next one and doing the same thing. His hands spread open her thighs, starting to slowly circle her already sore clit, and he gathered her juices on his fingers, bringing them to her lips. Emily blushed as he put his fingers, coated in her own juices, to her lips, but she opened her mouth to suck them clean. He pushed his fingers through her parted lips and over her tongue. She sucked on them until they were clean, and he groaned around her nipple, tugging with his teeth as he was careful that his fangs didn't pierce.

He then removed his fingers from her mouth, starting to put his fingers to her pussy lips again, spreading them wide to expose her wet hole. He started to push a single finger in, making her moan. Allen forced another in as he started to suck on her clit. She laid back, moaning as his fingers worked in and out of her pussy. He started to run his tongue over her clit. Emily could feel his tongue working over her as his fingers continued in and out of her, driving her closer and closer to another orgasm as she grabbed the silky sheets.

"That's right. Come for me." Allen teased her, and Emily bit her bottom lip, trying to keep from crying out.

She propped up to look at him, and her eyes started to flutter closed as she was lost in the pleasure that he was bringing her. His tongue played expertly over her clit, and his words sent a shiver through as she started to arch from the bed. She couldn't help it as another orgasm ripped through her, and she cried out in pleasure. It was music to Allen's ears as he groaned, starting to shift a little.

He couldn't help it when his hand came around to grip his own cock, wanting to push into her until he climaxed inside of her. *Soon.* He thought, but for now he just slid his fingers out of her. He teased her slit by letting his tongue slide over her, diving into her hole to collect her juices as she swallowed them. Emily was now propped up and dazed as she looked at his red eyes, but she ignored it, too lost in the pleasure to think that she was seeing right.

His powers grabbed her, and even without them, she wouldn't have cared so long as Allen continued. Allen stood up, and he slid her by her hips to the edge of the bed as she propped up. Her ample breasts jiggled when she did, and he reached out to tug on her nipple again.

She was too dazed to do anything more than moan, arching into his hand. She wanted him to continue, and she started to push back against Allen the moment he started to line his twitching, hard cock up with her wet, sensitive pussy before he pushed just the tip of his cock in. He moved it in and out, teasing her as he forced her to stretch around the tip but leaving her empty.

She groaned, trying to fuck back against him to make him take her, but Allen kept his hands at her hips, stopping her from doing so. She couldn't help but to groan, and he started to teasingly fuck just a little more into her, inch by inch with each thrust, going slow enough to keep teasing her. His cock arched in a way that started to hit her g-spot when he was a little over halfway in. then, Allen pulled all the way back to where Emily was just stretched out around the head before he slammed back in. His balls slammed against her as she cried out in pleasure, eyes closed as he forced her to stretch around him.

"That's right..." He groaned, starting to fuck in and out of her.

"Take my cock." He continued, emphasizing each word with a thrust as Emily tried to grind her hips against him.

Emily was lost in the pleasure. it seemed like every nerve ending she had was on fire, and she could feel the way that the sheets rubbed against her naked body, and she wrapped a heel clad foot around his back, pulling him in by the waist so that he'd thrust harder.

"Fuck me." Emily groaned, too lost in the pleasure that he was bringing her to think about anything else as he started to thrust a little harder.

A little deeper, as she continued to try to fuck back against him. His thumbs rubbed circles in her hips, pulling her to meet each thrust. Not that it was necessary. Emily was more than eager as her pussy started to clench around his cock, twitching as he got closer and closer to his own climax. She could feel his cock head reaching all the way back to her cervix and hitting her g-spot with each thrust as she cried out in pleasure.

Chapter Six

Allen knew he couldn't last much longer, and he started to hammer in and out of her pussy, making her groan. Emily could feel each and every thrust, and his groans were just driving her closer to another climax while he continued driving into her already sore, overly sensitive pussy. She didn't know if she could come again so soon, and yet Allen was driving her towards another orgasm as reality hit her.

She knew she was on a stranger's bed after he had kissed her, and there was a large part of her that couldn't understand how she had ended up there. She looked up at the man that was giving her so much pleasure, and Emily was immediately lost in those eyes with just a hint of impossible red. She started to clench around his cock all over again, throbbing around him as she got close to her own climax before Allen slowed down again.

She whimpered, and when she glanced up, she could see that he was smirking. She knew that he was keeping her on the edge of another orgasm on purpose, and yet there was nothing she could do but whimper and moan through her parted lips as she arched up to grind against him. He started to pound into her harder again, and Emily could feel his nails digging in. They seemed sharper than she had imagined. She didn't know that Allen was fighting the beast inside of him, relishing in her cries of pain and pleasure.

"God. I'm going to come inside of you. I'm going to come in your tight fucking pussy like the dirty little slut you are." Allen groaned, and she couldn't help but to clench a little tighter around him at his words.

Allen couldn't hold off any longer as he started to come deep inside of her, making her groan as she felt his hot, thick come start to fill her wet, clenching pussy. She continued to twitch around him, still on the verge of her third orgasm which she couldn't achieve as he barely thrust inside of her. Allen enjoyed every twitch around him that milked his cock. He could feel himself depositing every drop inside of her before he pulled out his still hard cock to rub against her clit, making her groan.

Her orgasm had just slipped away, and yet he continued to tease her with his cock. She couldn't believe that he was still hard after coming inside of her, and he just smirked a little, tugging at her nipple to get her attention again. Allen loved to watch her pant as his come started to leak out of her pussy, but he knew he wasn't done with her yet. Not with his cock still throbbing in his hand, making him want to fuck into her all over again.

She moaned, still in post orgasm bliss, and he couldn't help it anymore. He started to massage her hips with his strong fingers, making her squirm under him as she lay there with her legs parted. His fingers flicked over her overly sensitive clit as Emily moaned a little louder, making her shudder in pleasure. He made sure she was looking him in the eyes, not bothering to hide his fangs anymore as they peaked out from his lips as he smirked.

"Do you think we're done?" He teased her, tracing his finger down her slit and back up again before flicking her clit, mixing pain and pleasure.

Emily couldn't help but to close her eyes as she groaned, arching up from the bed. She shook her head no, and there was a part of her that saw the fangs, but she was lost in pleasure. He helped her to sit up, his throbbing cock between them as his arms wrapped around her. Emily was pressed tight to his chest, and her wrapped around his neck.

He inhaled the scent of her hair, and the smell of her arousal and blood filled his senses. Allen knew that he couldn't hold on anymore as he swept her hair to the side, exposing her neck. He nipped at it gently, placing light kisses down the side before hitting right over the pulse point. He sucked on her neck as she moaned, squirming and grinding against his cock which was between them.

He couldn't take it anymore. Allen let his fangs slide into her soft neck, and he could taste the blood as it welled up to fill his mouth. Allen started to wiggle his hips, grinding his cock lightly into her stomach as his come started to leak from her. Emily felt her pussy clench as he bit her before a rush of endorphins hit her system, and her cry of pain turned to one of pleasure.

He sucked lightly on her neck, making sure not to drink too deeply, but the way she pressed into his fangs was almost too much. Emily didn't know what happened when pleasure exploded through her after he bit her, but all she could think about was that pleasure which continued to course through her veins. It was almost too much, and she felt on the verge of coming all over again as her whole world started to spin.

Her eyes fluttered closed, and she could feel warmth flooding the area he bit as he drank down something she didn't want to think about. If she didn't know any better, Emily would have sworn it was blood, and yet there was a part of her mind that wouldn't allow her to process that. He nipped gently before tracing his tongue over the two puncture marks after sliding his fangs from her. She was still on an endorphin rush, and she was like clay in his hands as she still hung her arms around him limply with a smile on her face.

As he pulled back, Emily got a full view of the man before her through her hazy pleasured state, and she saw dark red eyes and fangs. *Vampire.* Is the only thing that went through her mind, and she knew she should be terrified. Yet, all she could do was clench a little at the thought of Allen taking her again. Her mind refused to process anything else.

Chapter Seven

Allen helped Emily to stand up before turning her around, pressing her face to the bed as her hips pressed to the edge. She was standing on her high heels with her curvy round ass high in the air for him. Allen felt his cock twitch all over again, and he traced kisses down her back, leaving small traces of her blood. She shivered as he started to massage her plump ass cheeks, making her push back against him, standing fully on her heels now as her hardened nipples dragged over the silk covers.

She groaned as he started to slide his cock back into her wet pussy, pumping in and out a few times before pulling back out. He started to slide his cock all the way in before pulling all the way back, parting her ass cheeks with his hands as his nails dug into her sensitive flesh. Emily groaned as he started to push his throbbing hard cock against her tight, puckered asshole.

She groaned, but Emily was too relaxed and lost in the pleasure that Allen was bringing her to protest too much. He started to push into her tight, puckered asshole as it clenched, trying to keep him out. As his head popped in, he moaned in pleasure. Emily clenched around him, squirming slightly, but Allen leaned over her, nipping at her shoulder as she started to relax.

"That's right. Relax. Let me into your tight ass." He groaned, as he started to feed every inch of his throbbing cock into her tight, puckered hole.

She whimpered again, seeming too lost in the pain mixing with the pleasure, but Allen reached down to rub her clit. She started to relax around him, and Allen slammed home. His balls slapped against her wet pussy as he was balls deep in her ass. Her tight passage gripped his cock like a glove, making her squirm as he started to pull back just an inch or two before slamming home again.

Allen then pulled his cock all the way out until just the tip of his cock was gripped by her anal ring, and she groaned as he started to grind his hips, fucking back into her. Allen couldn't stop it anymore, he wanted to come. Allen fucked into her harder, making her groan as she bounced with each and every thrust. Her nipples dragged against the sheets, and every nerve she had felt like it was on fire as she clenched around him.

Her pussy was already wet again and dripping juices. Her hand slid underneath her and between her legs as she started rubbing her clit again, adding more pleasure to the mix. He started to thrust a little harder, and Emily could still feel his cock twitching in her as with each and every thrust. Allen knew that he couldn't hold on much longer, and he started to thrust a little deeper but just as quick.

She couldn't help it anymore, as she groaned. He started to go over the edge, pushing all the way in so that he could start to splatter his come inside of her. At the last minute, he pulled out, leaving her ass gaping as the rest of his load splattered over her round ass cheeks. Emily knew she was so close, and yet it seemed like Allen was going to leave her on the edge. She whimpered a little as she felt his come splatter over her ass cheeks after filling her.

He smacked her ass before sliding two fingers deep into her pussy, sending Emily over the edge into another orgasm as she collapsed on the bed. Her knees bucklered underneath her. He watched as Emily panted, and his hunger got the best of him again as he helped her up after a moment to perch on the end of the bed. He swept her up in a kiss, his lips moving against hers as his tongue pressed over her own in a dance that sent her shivering.

She was too exhausted and in too much bliss to say or do anything besides kiss him back, even as she once again looked into his deep, blood red eyes. Emily could feel his fangs graze her bottom lip as he nipped at it, causing it to bleed a little. He took the other side of her neck, kissing down it again as she shivered under him, with moans passing through her parted lips. She was beautiful, but all he could think about right now was his hunger as he scraped his fangs over her delicate flesh before biting in.

More endorphins rushed her system as she cried out, and soon enough the pain turned to pleasure. Emily relaxed against him before he pulled out, forcing himself not to drink too much as she looked up at him with a smile on her face. There was still that part of her trying to reason out everything she had just done, but she couldn't deal with it anymore. She didn't want to see anything besides a hot billionaire in front of her, and she was enjoying the feeling that he had given her. Emily couldn't help it anymore.

She passed out into oblivion soon after, and Allen smiled down at her happily. He looked at her with a smile on his face as he helped get her into the bed the rest of the way, gently taking off her heels before heading off to the shower. He ran his fingers through his hair as the red faded from his eyes and his fangs started to shrink. She wouldn't really believe it in the morning, and there was no evidence for her to see. He smiled as he stepped into the hot water after a long day of hunting.

Chapter Eight

Emily woke up with the worst hangover she had ever had. It seemed like her head was pounding, and she could have sworn that she didn't drink that much. For a moment, she didn't even want to open her eyes. She just groaned silently for a second before allowing them to open, and that's when she looked around, taking in her surroundings.

She hadn't expected to see the beautiful suite and herself tucked beneath the covers. That's when it all came flooding back to her, and she started to blush. Her holes were sore along with other muscles in her body. She couldn't help but to shake her head. Looking around, she didn't see Allen at all, and she couldn't help but to frown. Did he leave after sex? She thought, but that's when she saw the note next to the bed. She grabbed.

Just order something to get you started. I talked to your manager about you being late, and call whenever you want. 948-284-2795.

~A

For a moment, she couldn't help but to think that it was really sweet, but then she groaned. *You talked to my manager?* She thought, and Emily couldn't help but to be mortified at whatever he had said. A large part of her didn't want to go anywhere at all. *No less to work.* So, instead she decided to take him up on that offer, and she ordered room service while being thankful that she barely knew any of the kitchen staff.

She smiled as she turned on the TV, looking around for her clothes. After finding them, she shook her head, sighing. That's when Emily caught sight of the luxury shower she had been dying to try, and a grin spread over her face before she started to head that way. Stepping into the steaming water, it felt like all her troubles started to melt away, and the soap smelled heavenly.

She took a moment to enjoy a luxury she could rarely ever afford. *And never in such nice of a room.* All too soon she knew the food would be coming, and so she wrapped a towel around her before she heard the door unlatch. She stood there, eyes widening as a very cleanly dressed and smirking Allen stared back at her. Her eyes were wide, and she couldn't help but to look for red eyes and fangs that couldn't be there as the thought flooded back to her. Emily tried to shake it away, telling herself it was impossible as she clutched the towel tighter.

"You just said I could enjoy myself, and I really thought I should clean up before breakfast." She started to ramble before stopping herself by biting her bottom lip. He couldn't help but to chuckle a little, and it sent a shiver of excitement through her that she just didn't want to admit to.

"I believe the first time you saw me in a towel." He said lazily, shaking his head with that arrogant smile still plastered over his face. She couldn't help but to just bite her lip, waiting to hear what he was going to say next.

"I believe the tables have turned." Allen said, closing the distance between them before he tilted her chin up so that she was looking at him.

His lips captured hers in a kiss, and he could feel his hunger starting to come back already, but he pushed it down. His lips moved gently against Emily's, who was already moaning into the kiss in a way that made him want to take her right then and there. When he broke the kiss after caressing her tongue with his own and nipping at her bottom lip, Allen went to whisper hotly in her ear.

"I believe breakfast can wait." Allen said as he found the edge of her towel, pulling at it until it dropped to the floor. Emily was once again naked before him, and he groaned a little. He could already smell her arousal, and his own cock started to harden as she smiled up at him. She kissed him again, and he was taken aback as he wrapped his arms around her before picking her up. Allen carried her back into the showers, and she knew she was in for a round two where she'd be delightfully sore all over again.

The End

The French Billionaire

Billionaire Romance

By: Lisa Cartwright

☐ **Copyright 2015 by Lisa Cartwright - All rights reserved.**

In no way is it legal to reproduce, duplicate, or transmit any part of this document in either electronic means or in printed format. Recording of this publication is strictly prohibited and any storage of this document is not allowed unless with written permission from the publisher. All rights reserved.

Respective authors own all copyrights not held by the publisher.

Chapter One

Emily Goodson's journey into French culture started with a phone call from her sister, Lynette. After the usual pleasantries, Lynette said, "Something came up which helps both of us. You need work in your area. I need someone inside a certain business. Someone with your talents and equipment fits exactly. It shouldn't be dangerous, but I'd keep my head up if I were you."

Emily took down the information. She was going to be applying for a job with a small company that dealt in paintings.

As she gets ready for her interview, she realizes she has to take the mirror out of the closet. It wasn't easy for her. She gathered her courage and retrieved the full length mirror and set it against a wall.

Facing away from the mirror, Emily prepared herself like a knight putting on armor. First, her pretty panties from Victoria's Secret. They were a lovely shade of blue and cut like a bikini. She'd never had that kind of panty before. She'd always used the full variety.

She held her breath and turned around. There she was and the sight didn't make her want to cry. She turned from side to side and smiled. She turned all the way around and looked over her shoulder and smiled. No cellulite, no flab, not mottled or discolor skin. Her body looked fantastic' curvaceous and full.

She moved her eyes above her waist. Her breasts had always pleased her. Even when she was so heavy, they never drooped or fell. Always buoyant, always shaped as if they belonged in a man's hand. She knew they were her best feature. She'd shopped online for just the right bra and found a demi bra from a French company that fit perfectly. It pushed her breasts up just the right amount to give her some fullness in a top with a low neckline without making her look cheap.

She slipped into the skirt and a top with a scoop neckline. She turned around and smiled again.

In the previous year, Emily lost over a hundred pounds. Her new body was round and firm. Her brother told her that her body was perfect for a man who liked to grab something and hold on.

The address took her to a long empty street in the hills above Malibu. The street ended in a cul-de-sac with one building. She parked, got out of the car and stared. It was a Queen Anne mansion that stretched for two hundred feet in front of her. Four separate towers lifted off the main building. Each roof had a weather vane of a different style.

She climbed the stairs and rang the bell. The man who answered the door appeared out of breath, as if he had been somewhere far away from the door. He said, "Good morning. May I help you?" Emily had never heard a butler speak with a French accent. In his mouth, it sounded foreign, not to the country but to the job, as if a poet were working a road crew.

Emily said, "Yes. I'm Emily Goodson. I'm applying for the job of curator. I'm supposed to talk with Mr. Latrec."

"Please follow me."

The man was tall and stocky. He wore a black suit and tie and looked perfect for the role of butler. As Emily walked behind him she glanced in each room they passed. Paintings by artists she revered hung in every room. She hoped they were all fakes. Any house with as many perfect paintings as this would be a prime target for thieves.

The man led her into a kitchen. He took off his coat and got a clean apron from a hook on the wall. Another man stood at a stove big enough to service a restaurant. The man she followed said, "I am back now. You may stop stirring." He took the spoon away from the other man and examined whatever was cooking with a practiced eye. "Bon. You did a good job this time. The béchamel is perfectly blended. Bon."

The man stepped away from the stove and turned to Emily. He said, "Good morning. I am Reynard Latrec. This is my home and my office. I'm guessing my chef didn't introduce himself. His name is Alain Lefevre. Say hello, Alain." Alain didn't look up from the sauce. He lifted his hand in the air and waved two fingers. Reynard continued, "Please have a seat at the table. Have you eaten?"

Emily smelled the wonderful aroma of a perfectly cooked sauce.

"No. I haven't."

"We'll be eating in a few minutes. Please stay with us for lunch." Emily saw a rather naughty smile light up Reynard's face. He turned to Alain and said, "Would it be too much trouble to add one more for lunch, mon ami?"

Alain and Reynard had played this game before. Alain turned, not to Reynard, but to Emily. "For a woman of such obvious beauty and culture, it is always a pleasure to add another setting to the table." He turned to Reynard and sniffed. Reynard raised one eyebrow in response. He turned to Emily. "Do you have any questions about the job?"

Emily looked at Reynard for the first time with nothing else to distract her. She saw a man six feet tall, husky without fat, and handsome in the way of Frenchmen; perfect features arranged with a casual hand and lively. Somewhere deep inside her, something stirred. She said, "If I understand the job listing, you want a curator to handle a moderate collection of paintings. The collection will be constantly revised with new additions and deletions and must be kept current and accurate."

"Exactly right. I live by buying and selling art. I am always finding something I believe is undervalued and selling it for a profit. The paperwork and provenance must be accurate and up-to-date."

A new voice came from behind Emily. A woman said, "Finally, you hire someone to do the housekeeping for the paintings. I am sick of doing it. My own work suffers. Who is this new addition?" The owner of the voice walked over to the table. She was pretty, thin with a sharp nose and angry blue eyes. She looked like she'd smelled spoiled milk a week earlier, and it stayed with her. She looked at Emily without extending her hand for a greeting. "You look like you can do the job. Stand up. Let me look at you."

Reynard said, in reproach, "Mignon. This is unseemly."

Mignon didn't look at Reynard, instead she waited for Alain to say something. He tended to his sauce.

Emily stood up. She remembered not to smooth her clothes or fidget. Mignon looked her up and down then cast a glance at Alain again. He continued with the sauce. Mignon said, "You have a body made for men to hold. I approve. However, you should know that Mr. Latrec is completely off limits. He is your employer."

Reynard stood up. "Mignon. That crosses the line of good behavior. Stop it."

Mignon looked tragic and lonely. She snarled, "I will not have women come into this home and office making the plays for your attention. It is distracting and wrong." She folded her arms. "There. I have said my pieces and I have done. Do what you will."

Alain didn't look up from the sauce. He said, "'Piece', mon petit chou chou (my little cabbage, a term of endearment). You say 'I have said my piece' not 'pieces'."

Mignon raised her nose in the air. "The cook corrects my English yet again. Very well. I am capable of change." She huffed. "In any events, I have made my say. I will get back to work." She turned to Emily. "Welcome to the family." She caught sight of Alain's upraised finger. "What is it, mon petit cuire (my little cook)? Have I said the wrong again?"

Alain moved the pot off the burner. He turned to look at Mignon.

Emily gasped. She hadn't looked at him before with clear eyes. He must have been six foot six inches tall, thick and well muscled. His voice was low and cultured. He said, "Why must you behave so, Mignon? With all of the drama?"

Mignon had been simmering before, just below the boil so that she bubbled enough to shake the lid on her pot. Now, she exploded into face-reddening fury. She sputtered, "You... You cook. You correct me so often and never tell me when I say it right. You treat me as if I were a piece of furniture. It is maddening to have a man such as you around. I will stand it no longer. I will work from my room for the rest of the day. I have spoken." She stomped over to the door and opened it.

Alain said, "Lunch is ready. We have Bouchée à la Reine. The sauce is perfect."

Mignon didn't turn around. "Did you increase the onion and make less on the nutmeg?"

"Yes."

"Very well. I will eat then I go to my room to wall myself off from the rest of you." She sat at the table.

Reynard brought Emily back to the conversation. "Miss Mignon Budreau is our technician. She repairs the damage time has done to our works of art. Now, tell me about your qualifications."

Emily listed them in order of importance. She'd done it before, and it worked.

Reynard nodded. "Excellent. The job pays..." He listed a figure a third again higher than any job Emily had heard of in her field. He continued, "It comes with full benefits and vacation. Will you take it?"

Emily had sense enough not to stand on the table and shout, "By damn, you bet your sweet ass I'll take it." She nodded. "I'd love to."

Reynard said, "Excellent. You can start tomorrow if that is convenient." He turned to Alain. "Tell any other applicants that the job is filled."

Mignon said to Emily, in a voice that demanded an answer, "What do you know of law enforcement and security?"

Emily froze for a second or two. They weren't supposed to know who she was.

Both men said, "Mignon." She held up her hand. "No. I will not be quiet on this point. We have paintings worth millions in a house that boasts a security system a full six decades old. We are an excellent target. Should I withhold my comments and feel sorrow at your graves that I didn't raise my voice? No." She glanced at Emily with suspicion. "Miss Goodson has qualifications that cover her field. That is good. But if we are broken into, will she be of value."

Emily breathed a sigh of relief. She could simply tell the truth, about this, at least. She said, "I did an internship on security and security systems with the L.A. County Art Museum. My real qualification comes from my father who is a policeman and my two brothers and one sister who are policemen and the many discussions

I have listened to growing up in a house full of cops. Also, I am certified to carry a concealed weapon and have qualified with the pistol in the LAPD reserve force. I will be happy to come to my job armed, if you wish."

Mignon nodded. "That is good. For myself, yes, bring the pistol with you every day. Someone should be able to keep me alive in case of trouble."

Reynard said, "You should have listed that on your resume."

"Yes, I should."

Alain said, "Lunch is served. Prepare yourselves." He placed four individual plates in front of Reynard, Emily and Mignon and the empty chair. He announced, "Bouchée à la Reine. Chicken breasts with morel mushrooms and onions. We will eat it with white wine and the béchamel sauce I prepared." He placed four dishes with a simple salad and bottles of oil and vinegar in the center of the table.

Conversation stopped as they concentrated on the food. In fifteen minutes, it was gone and all sat back and wiped their mouths on the linen napkins by their plates.

Emily said, "That was magnificent. Alain, you are a wizard." She happened to glance at Mignon when she said the words. Mignon glowed with pride.

Chapter Two

Emily signed some documents and left the incredible mansion. She drove past a car parked down the road a hundred yards. It demanded attention. Even in Los Angeles, a city known for conspicuous consumption, a Lamborghini Sesto Elemento stands out. Lamborghini extended itself for the Sesto Elemento. Built mainly of carbon fiber, the Sesto Elemento weighs only 2,200 pounds, no more than a small Volkswagon, and sports a V10 engine of 570 horsepower. It uses Prosaic heatproof glass to form the exhaust system and can run from zero to sixty in 2.5 seconds. It costs $2.2 million. It looks like someone put good aerodynamics on a shark.

Emily saw the driver of the car standing in the six foot high underbrush, looking back at the house with binoculars. She took a quick image with her phone and drove home.

The next day, Reynard showed Emily her desk and computer and the rooms in which the paintings were hung.

As they toured the huge home, Reynard said, "Are you from Los Angeles?"

"Yes. I was born in Hollywood and raised in the valley. You're French obviously. Your English is excellent. When did you arrive in the United States?"

Reynard opened his mouth to speak and paused.

She knew when someone was lying because it had been discussed over dinner. People telling the truth don't have to prepare beforehand. They simply go into a description of the event. It doesn't flow smoothly. When they lie, they've prepared their statements before they say them. It flows without error and sounds like a speech.

Reynard said, in words that came out without hesitation, "I came here when I was seventeen. I attended school in New York and graduated from NYU. My family has been in art for six generations. They're in New York City. I have three brothers and a sister." As an afterthought, he added, "I wish I could see them more often.

Emily asked, "Do you know anyone who drives a Lamborghini Sesta Elemento?"

Reynard looked down and shook his head. "No. I wish I did. I'd ask to borrow it." He rushed along to get to the next room.

Twenty minutes later, Reynard asked Emily to sit at her computer while he showed her the software for processing acquisitions. Emily noticed that Reynard hovered near her. She's worn a very expensive fragrance that day in case he got close enough to smell her. She could feel his breath on her neck.

She, very carefully, turned her head to ask him a question about the software. He, just as carefully, turned toward her. Their lips were within an inch of each other. She glanced down at his lips. He began to lean toward her then, at the last second, turned his head toward the screen.

They played this game for a month. Emily did her job with admirable skill and dedication and tried to get as close to Reynard as possible. Reynard obviously enjoyed the game. But they never actually touched.

Chapter Three

Mignon and Alain continued mostly ignoring each other except when Mignon had a tantrum and Alain intervened

It all changed on a rare Saturday when Emily had to work.

She was walking down a stairway when she looked out a window and saw Reynard and the suspicious man who drove the expensive Lamborghini talking in the back yard. She snapped an image on her cell phone.

At three in the afternoon, Mignon finally got what she had been asking for all along. Everyone was feeling a little hungry and out of sorts because dinner was still hours away.

Mignon said, very bluntly, "I quit. I can not work this way. I am never paid the attentions. I am always pushed off to the side in favor of Emily. I will leave tonight. It must be done. My life can't be lived under these condition." She'd started her speech speaking shrilly and ended it in a full screech.

Reynard said, "No, my sweet. This office is more a home than it is a workplace. You will not leave. You are a member of the family." He opened his arms and Mignon glided into them for a hug.

She left his arms and glared at Alain. She sputtered, "Here is a man. He takes me in his arms and tends to my feelings. Thank the Good God there is one man in the room."

Alain threw his kitchen gloves on the table and turned around. He said, "Enough." His voice was soft and the tone firm. He advanced on Mignon.

Mignon looked at him with concern as he towered over her. She said, "Alain? What are you going to do? Whatever it is, you can't do it. I must have my dignities. You can not take those away from me."

He didn't answer. He grabbed her left hand out of the air and pulled. He bent over to catch her on his shoulder as she fell forward. He walked to his bedroom with Mignon limp, hanging down his back. She said angry things in French at the top of her lungs. He held her in place with his arm over the back of her legs, under her skirt.

Reynard called after them, "Bon Chance, mon ami. Bon Chance."

Alain didn't answer or turn around. He waved two fingers over his head. Reynard and Emily noticed that Mignon was pounding on his back and demanding to be put down.

Chapter Four

Alain placed an incensed Mignon on her feet by his bed. She sputtered, "What do you think you are doing to me? Why have you carried me off in such a way? Over your shoulder with my legs showing and my skirt up to my rear end." She glanced down at his hands. "What are you doing now?"

Alain was undoing the buttons on her blouse. "I will not live with you the way you are, and I will not let you go."

"And do you think taking my clothes off will make me pleasant and calm like some fat Provence housewife on a farm?"

"That and my touch on your skin. No man is touching you. No one is giving you good feelings. I think that is the cause of this constant temper" He opened her blouse and pulled it from her skirt.

He pushed it off her shoulders. His hands moved slowly and carefully. He paused to study her lovely, lace bra and the breasts it contained.

Her voice gained volume and stridency. "Do you think I will change just because you roll me in the hay? Is that it?" She shook her finger in Alain's face. "Let me tell you something, my friend with muscles. It will take more than that to make me cheerful."

"I know that. If you will be quiet for a moment and let me do what must be done, I will tell you what more there is."

She perked up and waited. He didn't expand on his comment.

Alain rested his hands on her ribs below her bra. He looked her in the eye and moved his hands under her bra, lifting it over her breasts and up on her chest. He filled his hands with her modest, but shapely breasts. Her eyelids fluttered.

She put the back of her hand on her forehead. "Is this the way a gentleman acts? You overpower me with your greater size and take my boobs for your own."

"No, my sweet. Not that ugly word. I have my hands on your breasts. That shows proper respect for your beauty."

She dropped her hand. "Well, so what? What difference if you touch my boobs or my breasts? You don't have permission to do either one." She looked down at his hands. She felt their warmth against her skin. Alain lifted them up her chest slightly and gave them a squeeze. She said, "I say again, is this the way a gentleman acts towards a lady of delicacy?"

"Probably not. But it is what I'm doing to you now. And, unless you force me, I won't stop doing it."

"Until what? You aren't thinking that I will tolerate your body inside mine. That is too much. A woman of breeding wouldn't agree to that under any circumstances. Why don't you do the normal thing? Take me to dinner, bring me flowers and candy."

"Would you have agreed to a dinner such as you describe in a good restaurant? Would you keep still during such a dinner and not have the screaming tantrum?"

"Well, perhaps not, but it would have been nice to be asked." Her mouth grew firm. "But that is not the question we have. You are doing this without my permissions. How do you answer that?"

His voice rose. "Without your permission is it? Are you calling for help? Are you slapping my face and trying to get away? You are not."

"That doesn't mean I want you inside my body." She gasped. "What are you doing now?"

Alain found the zipper and clasp at the waist of her skirt. He dealt with it quickly and adroitly. Her skirt fell to the floor. She wore her bra under her arms, panties of a dangerous cut and translucency and thigh high stockings. She stepped out of her skirt. Alain picked it up and folded it. He put it over the back of a chair.

Mignon unhooked her bra and threw it on the same chair. She held up her hand. "Stop. We must put a hold on these proceedings. We will not be going… what is the American phrase?… Yes, we will not be going all the way, but no woman of any femininity will stand before a man without covering for her breasts and not demand an opinion. Do you like my breasts, Alain Lefevbre? Speak now. I must know."

Alain kissed the top of her left breast.

She said, "At least, I can see that you appreciate me. That is good. But this must stop. Look a little longer to make sure you never have to do this again, and I will get dressed, and we can pretend that today is a fantasy."

Alain shook his head. "No, mon cherie. We must go far enough to make a change in your behavior, which is most abominable. As I look at it now, that means all the way." He bent his knees and wrapped his arms around her thighs. He lifted her up in the air. She squealed. "Now what are you doing?"

"Taking the next step. Notice please, that I have positioned you in my arms around your body at such a height that your lovely nipples and my mouth are the same."

Her voice was suspicious. "Why does that matter?" Her mouth dropped open and her hands clamped over her breasts. "You wouldn't put your lips on my nipples would you? That is a liberty I have not granted."

Alain stopped moving. He didn't talk. He didn't plead or beg. He looked into her eyes and waited. Mignon realized that he was a solid, stable man with strength she hadn't known about. She realized he wasn't going to let her down until he got what he wanted. She said, "I see I have no choice. I can't stay up here forever. I have work to do. Be nice. No biting and after this, I put my clothes on and leave. This is all you get." She dropped her hands slowly.

Alain opened his mouth and set it gently over her left breast. She jumped when his tongue touched her. He said, "That wasn't biting."

"You could have been preparing to bite."

"No. You said no biting and no biting is what we shall do."

He put his mouth back where it had been. He sucked and licked both nipples. He did it slowly and carefully. She made small noises that sounded like approval. Each nipple responded to his efforts by growing longer and harder.

He covered his teeth with his lips and pressed down gently on her right nipple then moved his jaw back and forth to give it a twist. He felt her skin heat up and watched, from up close, as it turned from a delicate, light color to pink then deep red. She moaned when he did it again. She whispered, with her eyes closed, "That feels like biting."

Alain noticed that her hand had moved from his shoulder to the back of his head and she was guiding his head back and forth from one to the other.

She moaned again. "This is not fair. You're not taking me by force, but I have no choice. You've incapacitated me by lifting me in the air, and you're having your way with me. My body is responding against my wishes. You know that soon I will not be able to fight back."

"That's true. Soon, we arrive."

Her eyes sprang open. "What do you mean 'arrive'? I told you we would not be taking this to its conclusion. When I give myself to a man, I want to be in charge. I'm not in charge of you. You don't obey orders. Now, we must stop."

He looked up at her. "What are you afraid of?"

She looked all around the room without answering the question.

He said, "Do you think to find an answer in a corner of the ceiling, perhaps behind the bed or under the chair?"

"What I am afraid is not your concern?"

Alain allowed her to slip through his arms until his hands found her lovely rear end. Her skirt didn't follow the rest of her body and bunched around her waist. He said, "My sweet, it is very much my concern. Why do you think I have hesitated to do this? I don't want to live with a shrew, but I can't live without you. So I have decided on this course of action. I can think of no other way to change our lives. You would run away if I gave you the chance." He paused. She watched him with worry in her face. He continued, "If I did nothing, sooner or later, you would run away in actuality, and I would lose you." He filled his hands with her panty covered body. She tried to dislodge his hands and couldn't budge them. He moved, first one hand then the other, inside her panties so that he held her perfect butt, skin to skin. She wiggled to make him let go. He didn't.

He tilted her over on the bed, slowly and with painful gentleness, on her back. His hands were in the perfect spot to slip inside the waistband of her panties and pull them off her legs. She gasped. "Alain! What are you doing?"

"I'm taking your lovely panties off, Mignon. I'm doing what must be done for us to be together."

He reached between her legs toward her pussy. Her hand was quicker. She covered her fragrant garden with her hand. "Stop. Please. All of what has happened up till now has been fun and games.

Touching me between my legs puts us across a line of some kind. How do you say it?"

"When I touch you, I will have crossed a line."

"Bon. What you said." She looked in his eyes then looked away. Her voice as she said her next words sounded disconnected, as if the woman who spoke them couldn't bear to own them. "You can't do that unless you're willing to stay with me forever. It is too much to ask for me. To let you have that liberty and not be assured of your presence in my life." She swallowed and swallowed again.

"I know that."

"No. You still don't have it completely. You're assuming I will become pleasant and agreeable. What if I don't. Will you stay with me if I still persist in complaining and screeching? What if you succeed in getting inside me with your big penis, and you give me a baby? Will you be there to help?"

Alain found her eyes with his. He was serious. "Did you know that Reynard and I are both of the military?"

"No. I didn't." She hadn't moved her hand. It was still a barrier to his progress.

"We were with the Commandos Marine in Afghanistan. We don't take on a responsibility and let it go afterwards. It is not in our nature."

For the first time, Mignon showed herself, naked and vulnerable. She crossed her chest with her arm, hiding her exposed, defenseless breasts. "Please. Take care of me. Don't leave me. I will let you go forward because I love you. And... and..." Alain allowed her pause to continue until she said, "...because I have wanted you to do this from the day I stepped into your kitchen. But you must promise. Will you take care of me as a husband should?"

Alain smiled at her. "I will. Until we occupy two plots in the cemetery, side-by-side."

She moved both hands. They lay on the bed, palms up, by her head. Alain kissed her once more to tell her that he appreciated her sacrifice.

His fingers found her pussy and stroked her delicate tissues. She closed her eyes and smiled. "Yes. Like that. You will make a good husband and lover."

"Mon Cherie, I have never asked you to marry me."

"You will." She put her fingers on his lips. "I don't have to pretend any more. I want you to love me and maybe give me a baby to raise. But we must do it without words. I need to feel everything you do to me. I can't if I have to listen to you talk."

Alain chose the best way of responding to her words. He kissed her again with commitment and love. She kissed back.

He backed off a few inches. "You said 'no words', but these are required at this point. I love you. I will love you no matter who you choose to be. That is permanent."

She surprised Alain by drawing him close and bursting into tears. She raised her face toward the ceiling and wailed in joy and relief. She stroked his cheek with hers. "You love me. I have wanted to hear those words for so long."

"I'll say them again. I love you. I love you. I love you."

While he talked he moved the head of his cock into her entrance. As he said the last three words, he slid gently inside her.

Mignon arched her back. "Oh you are big. How heavenly."

He moved them around until they laid on their sides. He brought her knee over to rest on his waist. H kept himself from moving any deeper and touched the delicate, sensitive tissues around her entrance. She closed her eyes and smiled. Alain noticed two tears on her cheeks. He kissed each one to wipe it away.

Alain didn't move for another ten minutes while he stroked and rubbed and pressed his hands against all of her important spots.

He felt her hips flex toward him convulsively and penetrated her slowly and relentlessly until he was completely buried. She crossed her arms over her chest and burrowed into his arms. Almost immediately, she pushed away from him. She rubbed her hands over his massive chest and arms. "You're so big and strong. I can depend on you." She lunged into him and stayed there. He wrapped her up and held her tightly.

He began a simple in and out movement she seemed to like. She made a light, quiet whimper every time he penetrated. Alain didn't change anything. Thirty minutes later, she arched her back and groaned. She beat his chest and arms with her hands and humped up against him with her hips. She gasped for air.

He felt her contract again and again inside her sheath. She gave a victorious cry and settled back into his arms.. She touched his cheek. "I am finished, mi amour. Now you. Inside me. I want a baby."

"As you wish."

Alain clasped her butt with both hands and brought her into his cock. He pumped her hips and his cock together ten more times. He pounded her body forcefully, slamming into her. All through the process, she looked calm and happy.

He clenched through his orgasm. She felt him pump his semen inside her hips.

He finished and all of the stiffening went out of him. She pulled him over on top of her. He covered her almost completely. Anyone looking down from above would see only her eyes over his shoulder and her legs below the knees.

He asked, "Am I too heavy?"

"No. I love your weight. It is perfect." She caressed his back with her hands. "You're here now, inside my arms. Stay. Be content. This is your home now."

Chapter Five

Emily called her sister, Lynette, when she got home. "Is there anyone involved in the drug traffic that drives a Lamborghini Sesto Elemento?"

"Yes. Ernesto Gomez. By the way, the car cost just three months of profits. He makes that much money."

Emily said, "I have to know something. I want to have more of a relationship with Reynard. I need to know if he's good or bad. I saw Ernesto outside Reynard's house a month ago and again talking with Reynard today. Can you tell me what's going on?"

The police, especially inside families, have a way of talking around the truth when there is something that must be conveyed and a reason not to tell everything. After a meaningful pause, Lynette said, "Does Reynard keep a number of paintings in his house?"

"Yes, he does. From what I understand, his security system isn't up to standard as well."

"Do you still have that small .380 pistol?"

"Yes."

Lynette's voice became firm, not concerned or worried, but firm. "I would move up to a .45. Choose one of the compact models. They're easier to carry." She paused. "Stop. I forgot about the two week waiting period. I'll be right over."

Lynette was two years younger than Emily. She was stocky because she had to be and blonde because she wanted to be. Ten minutes later, she knocked on the door.

When policemen and women are involved in something important and complicated, everything they say, how they say it and what they don't say has meaning. Lynette walked in and got the important things out of the way. She hugged her sister and examined her figure. She said, "Fantastic. You look wonderful. How does it feel?"

Emily blushed. "Exciting and good. What can you tell me about Reynard?"

Lynette wouldn't look at her. "I know him. He's helped us with some art thefts in the past."

"Is there something wrong with him?"

Lynette finally looked in Emily's eyes. She held out a package. "I brought this. Carry it with you anytime you're out of your apartment." She handed the heavy bundle to Emily.

Emily's voice shook a little. "Whenever I'm out of the apartment?"

"Yes. Are you still active in the LAPD reserves?"

"Yes."

Lynette took a deep breath. "The job sounds nice. I'm glad you've got it."

Emily frowned. "Enough talking around this. I want to fall in love with Reynard. Is he dirty?"

Lynette wouldn't answer directly. "Keep working for him and take your weapon to work and everywhere else from now on." She kissed Emily on the cheek. "I've got to leave. Come to dinner on Sunday."

Emily recognized a refusal to answer and didn't press it. "I will."

Chapter Six

Emily didn't like carrying a weapon where it could be seen. To her, it was an article of clothing and a tool of her trade, not a symbol of violence. She didn't need to show it off to bolster her image. Her blouses had strips of velcro along the opening in front. Emily used a holster that fit against her ribs above her waist and couldn't be seen in ordinary circumstances. She wore the holster and pistol from that point forward.

The next day gave her a decision to make. She didn't want to make it.

Reynard and she were studying a new acquisition, a minor canvas by Manet that had a good provenance. ('Provenance' means history. A work of art is authenticated by the substance of its known history as well as expert examination.).

They leaned over the painting. At some point Emily, leaned too far. She began to fall and grabbed Reynard for support. Reynard did what any man would do; he put his arms around her and brought her back to vertical.

He didn't take his arms away. In fact, he brought her closer. They looked at each from very close together.

Emily went over all of it in a flash. She remembered Lynette's hesitancy in her approval of Reynard. She also remembered that Lynette hadn't suggested she leave the job and him.

Most importantly, she smelled Reynard and felt his muscles and steadiness. She felt the pistol against her ribs and thought, "What the heck. I'm armed" and looked at his lips. He took the hint and kissed her. She felt helpless and vulnerable in his arms, and she liked it.

Emily got her first hint of the seriousness of the situation. Reynard didn't tell her about his emotions. He looked deep into her eyes and said, "I want you to take the afternoon off. Take Mignon and Alain with you and go to the beach."

She said, "First, before we leave each other's arms, kiss me again."

He did.

Chapter Seven

The three of them drove to Malibu. Emily put on a nice one piece suit that dipped low on top. Mignon almost wore a scandalous bikini that showed virtually all of her.

She and Alain made an interesting couple. Mignon attracted attention that evaporated when it met Alain's smoldering, glowering, six foot six inch frame. Mignon walked arm in arm with Alain and chattered happily.

They sat on the beach under an umbrella. Mignon in the middle.

It happened twenty minutes after they arrived. A series of loud bangs disturbed the sea air. Emily dove into her bag for her gun. Alain rolled over on top of Mignon who crawled underneath him. He whipped open a beach towel that had been wadded up by his side and produced a gun that made Emily's look like a toy. They lay on the sand sweeping the beach with their eyes for the source of the sound.

Three kids threw more firecrackers on the beach and ran away. Both guns retreated back into their hiding places and Mignon came out from under Alain.

They looked at each other with significance. Alain went back to his book. Mignon snuggled against him and Emily studied her iPad.

Emily didn't see anything on the screen. She needed to know what had transpired and why they handled it as they did. She thought, "Alain has a gun. Does he have it because he and Reynard are involved in something dangerous? How much does the art market provide for Reynard? He lives in a huge house. The taxes alone would break most fortunes. Lynette insisted that I carry a weapon all the time. That means I'm in danger. Am I supposed to be defending

Reynard and the others or protecting myself from Reynard and Alain? Why did Alain and Mignon accept the danger that just happened without a comment? Reynard kissed me. Do we have a future?"

When they got back to the house, Reynard greeted them, and they went back to work.

Chapter Eight

At four in the afternoon, Emily needed a document that was attached to a painting in the cellar. She walked down the stairs into the room that had the painting. A door in the room led to another room Emily had never seen. It was always locked. Reynard said it was empty.

That afternoon, the door was open. Emily heard voices coming from inside the room. She crept over and stood next to the door against the wall. She heard Reynard said, "One million for the trip. I won't do it for anything less."

A voice that was born south of the border and sounded like every bordello and back alley in the world said, "Then you won't do it. That's too much money." The voice paused. "Hombre, do you think

I'm that rich? I don't have money like that, and I can't get it. This operation won't produce it. Cut your price in half and we have a deal."

"Three quarters of a million."

"Bastardo. Hijo di Puta." The words carried no anger or belligerence. In fact, they were good natured. "Bien. Done. But you bear all responsibility for delivery. If it fails, you must make good."

"Done for me as well. Let's go upstairs to the map room. I'll show you how the deliveries will be made."

Emily froze. She heard footsteps coming from the room. Her glance at the door on the other side of the room told her she couldn't get to it without being caught. She stayed where she was.

The door next to her opened all the way. She was on the fortunate side of the door. It opened in front of her, hiding her from the two men.

Reynard and Ernesto walked through the room. She saw Reynard's head twitch and a hesitation in his stride, but he kept going. She remembered her perfume.

After they went through the door, Emily took her shoes off. She knew another way upstairs and a means of getting close enough to the map room to hear.

She bound out of the room, turned to her right and ran up four flights of stairs. She slipped into a room next to the map room. She saw immediately that the walls were too thick to hear anything and there were no doors connecting to the other room.

She stepped to the window and opened it.

She looked down and the scene swirled before her eyes. She moaned, "Why did it have to be heights? I hate heights."

The ledge along the side of the building was only a foot wide. She stepped out into thin air. The view was delightful. She could see all the way to the ocean. She could also see every foot of every floor directly below her. She inched along the ledge, being careful not to step in the bird droppings littering the ledge.

Inside the room, Reynard drew a faint line on a map from Los Angeles down the coast of Mexico to Columbia, out to the Caribbean then back . "We pick up the product in Colombia and make stops in the Bahamas, Bimini then back through the canal and up to these Mexican cities. This is the biggest cargo I have ever heard of. Seventeen tons of heroin. The danger is extreme."

"Yet, you will do it, will you not?"

"Yes. For that amount of money, I will."

Emily inched along the wall outside in the open air. The window in the map room was closed. She had to get right next to it to hear.

The wind came up suddenly and blew against her from the side. She leaned and tried to recover. Unfortunately, her flailing arm struck the side of the building and pushed her out into space.

She didn't hear the window open. She felt a hand grab her arm and rescue her.

Reynard pulled her into the room. "What have we here?"

She looked at his face. It wasn't the face of the man she loved. It was hard and cold.

He said, "A spy from the police."

Ernesto said, "Who is she, my friend?"

"My curator." He ran his hands over her body starting with her neck. "Are you hiding any listening devices or guns, my little girl?" He pressed his hands around and under her breasts then down her chest. She felt him touch the gun in its holster and move on. He was sliding his hands down her hips and legs when he stopped.

Emily had been looking out the window at freedom and safety. When his hands stopped, she looked down. Ernesto held his own gun at the back of Reynard's neck.

Ernesto said, "My friend, I am not so easily fooled. You agreed to a price far too low to be of any value and agreed to replace the cargo if it were lost. You weren't going to make that trip were you. You work for the police. Both of you." He pulled a phone from his back pocket and pressed a number. He said into the phone, "It is as I feared, Raoul. It is a police trap. Bring the car up to the front. I will lead my two captives out to the curb. I may have to kill the others in the house. Don't worry if you hear loud noises." He closed the connection and gestured with his pistol. "Up. You will walk ahead of me."

Reynard got to his feet. He looked at Emily with profound regret. "I'm sorry about this."

"It's not your fault."

Ernesto's voice interrupted them. "Stop. I am not an idiot. You searched the woman. I don't trust you. Get on your knees."

Reynard slowly dropped down again.

Emily heard a pistol slide into a holster then felt Ernesto's hands on her chest. He felt along her ribs then moved around to her front. He immediately clamped on her breasts. Emily thought, "Thank heavens for horny men." She wriggled as if she were trying to get him to let go. Her twisting and writhing brought her around so that the gun in her holster pointed at Ernesto. She slipped her hand inside her blouse. Without pulling the gun, she put her hand around the grip and pulled the trigger.

The noise in that small room was deafening. Emily wasn't able to turn enough to hit him in the chest. Her bullet grazed his side and surprised him. She pushed him off his feet and watched him fall.

By the time he landed, she had her gun out and pointed at his head. His hand moved toward his gun. Emily said, "Don't even think about it."

Reynard ran around the side and took Ernesto's gun. He ran to the window. The car that was going to take him and Emily to their death drove away.

Chapter Nine

That night, Reynard and Emily settled down on the couch to watch a silly television program. She kissed his cheek. "I'm so glad you're not a criminal."

"My dear, I'm glad you added that magnificent gun to your ensemble."

She turned to her side, facing him and moved her leg between his. She snuggled into his chest. She found the TV remote and turned it off. "What shall we do now?"

"Now that the police interviews are in the past, now that Alain and the newly calm Mignon have gone to their own bed, now that we are alone on a soft couch with only a few articles of clothing between us? I have no idea. What do you suggest?"

"Did Alain tell you that he and Mignon are getting married?"

"Yes. His tactic of pushing past her fears worked very well." He bent over and kissed her. "Shall I do that with you?"

"It seems a waste of energy. If you love me, you can have me right now, with my cooperation."

He paused. "Yes. I haven't said the words. I love you." He kissed her. "Do you not want the marriage vows first? It would make you more secure in your future."

She slid on top of him. She sat on his legs with her legs outside of his. She took off her blouse.

Emily said, "This is ruined. I hadn't looked at it before."

Outside their mansion, Manuel Aliva crept through the bushes. He'd looked forward to a significant payday after the aborted trip to the Caribbean. He resented the loss and the loss of his boss who, he knew, was giving him up to the police. He needed someone to kill to relieve his frustration. He crept to a ground floor window. He saw the woman sitting on the man's lap with her blouse off. He was a big fan of men's magazines. The woman had the figure he liked; full and smooth and with the kind of curves that made his palms itch. He took out a big gun and attached a silencer to the end of the barrel.

Emily held up her blouse. She poked a finger through the hole. Besides the hole, the fabric showed powder burns and smelled of gun smoke. She said, "It had to be one of my best."

She glanced down at Reynard to find him with his hands raised. "I surrender. You may do what you will to my body, but you will never get my heart." He looked at the pistol in her holster.

Emily unhooked and unwrapped the holster from around her rib cage and set it aside. She put his hands on her perfect, generous breasts and held them there. She said, with knowing complacency, "Reynard, I have weapons that make that gun look like a cap pistol."

Reynard nodded. "I know. I hold two of them now." He gave the soft mounds held captive in his hands a squeeze. He was too impressed to make jokes. "Would you remove you brassiere, please. I want to hold you without anything between my hands and your skin."

He surprised her. While she was unhooking her bra, he slid his hands under her skirt and up her legs. Her eyes went wide and she gasped. "I love it when you touch my bare skin. That feels so good."

He caressed her legs and looked at her breasts. He told her, "I'm going to ask you to marry me tomorrow. Will you say 'yes'?"

She put her hands behind his head and leaned forward to let him kiss her breasts. "Why don't you ask me now?"

In between little kisses and small sucking movements, he said, "Because we will have daughters. They will ask you how I proposed. Was I romantic? Did I make it special, bring you flowers and dance with you? I don't want you to have to tell them that we had just captured a criminal and decided to make love on the couch in front of the television set on which was running a regrettable episode of Gilligan's Island. You must have a proper tale to tell them. I want my daughters to think of me as a sensitive man."

He stopped talking and worked hard on her left nipple. She groaned. He ran his hand down her tummy inside her panties until he held her fragrant garden. He slid one finger inside her sheath and pressed the back of his thumb against her little button. She threw her head back and groaned louder. She managed to say, "Don't forget."

He said, "I won't" as he tilted her over on her back on the couch. He took his hands and her panties out from under her skirt. He stood up and started taking off his clothes. He stopped to flip her skirt up to her waist. "You are so beautiful."

"Thank you. That means more to me than you know." She rubbed her tummy and the inside of her thighs with her hands.

Manuel had a perfect view. His window looked into the room from below the couch. He could see between Emily's legs. He had to move quickly. He would kill Reynard then quickly cover the woman with his pistol. He had to threaten her enough to make her keep silent. Then he could take her as he wished.

Emily saw Reynard's erection and sat up. "You're wonderful. So big. Come over here. Your magnificent cock needs my attention." Reynard stood between her knees while she took him in her mouth and sucked. She added her hands along the shaft of his cock.

Reynard gave her a gentle push on the forehead. She leaned against the back of the couch and pulled her knees up to her shoulders. She said, "Turn about is fair play. I need to be kissed."

Reynard dropped to his knees and buried his nose in her private garden. She was as wet as a swamp. Her aroma drifted up to Reynard, went through his nose and into his soul.

He spent time stimulating the expressive, intricate tissues in her pussy. She moaned and her hips bucked against him. She dropped flat on the couch and opened her legs. Reynard moved between them and lowered himself.

Manuel nodded to himself. He whispered, "Now."

Another voice, a feminine voice, whispered, "No. Not now. Not ever." Manuel felt the steel of a gun barrel press against his head. A woman's arm slid down his and took the gun out of his hand. He felt a hand on his collar pulling him away from the window. The voice said, "No noise. Let the lovebirds have their privacy. They deserve it."

Reynard put the head of his cock into the entrance of Emily's sheath and pushed. She was wide and wet, and it took little effort to penetrate completely.

They rested for a moment. Reynard said, "May I ask you a personal question?"

Emily blushed. "You couldn't be more personal with me that you are right now. Go ahead."

"When was your last monthly cycle?"

"It ended two weeks ago. Yes. I am fertile. I know you aren't wearing a condom." She kissed him. "I would love to have your baby, even if we start it before we get married."

"Good, because you feel wonderful inside."

Reynard led her to her orgasm and waited while she humped and writhed and twisted. When she'd come out the other end, he said, "I will now put my semen inside you. Let us both hope for a child."

Emily said, "Oh yes. That would be so wonderful. Go ahead."

Reynard plunged and withdrew energetically for thirty seconds then pressed his hips against hers until he was completely buried inside her. He pumped his semen into her waiting sheath.

When he was done, he floated down on her. She felt his weight press her down into the couch gradually. She wrapped her arms and legs around him. "Welcome home, Reynard. Your family is glad to see you."

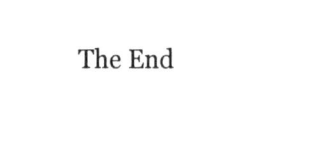

The Fallen Revenge

Billionaire Romance

By: Lisa Cartwright

☐ **Copyright 2015 by Lisa Cartwright - All rights reserved.**

In no way is it legal to reproduce, duplicate, or transmit any part of this document in either electronic means or in printed format. Recording of this publication is strictly prohibited and any storage of this document is not allowed unless with written permission from the publisher. All rights reserved.

Respective authors own all copyrights not held by the publisher.

Prologue

Mia Madison had now been staring aimlessly at her computer for the past forty-five minutes, scrolling between various social networking websites instead of doing anything remotely productive. Sure, her private detective service was a little slow at the moment, but she knew she should probably be organizing her case files or something. She was desperate for a new case, or any excuse to leave the office, really.

Just as she was thinking that maybe she should just leave work early today, she heard the tell-tale *ding* of a new email in her inbox. Her heart started to race with anticipation as she opened it. *Please be a new case, and not more junk mail,* she thought.

It was from a woman named Lillian Davis, who apparently thought her boyfriend was cheating on her and wanted to prove it. At first glance, Mia thought this seemed like a pretty standard case. But after reading the email more closely, she realized there was something different about it --- Lillian's philandering boyfriend was none other than Alexander Will, owner and CEO of Will Golden Corporation. Mia didn't usually follow the news, but even she knew who Alexander Will was: a young heir to one of the most successful companies in the world, completely rolling in money, and absolutely gorgeous. She also realized that Lillian Davis wasn't just anyone - she was heir to the Davis Mining Company fortune.

There was nothing Mia enjoyed more than taking down people who thought they had it all.

"This will be a win for the 99 percent," she thought. *"I'm in!"*

She emailed Lillian back right away to set up a meeting.

***

Chapter 1

Mia and Lillian had agreed to meet at the Hudson Diner because it was a quiet, unassuming little restaurant, somewhere Alexander and his posh crowd of friends and coworkers would never go. Plus, they had amazing waffles. The two young women sat down in a cozy booth near the kitchen, where they could chat privately.

Mia's first impression of Lillian was that she was beautiful in a very worldly sort of way. Mia herself was often considered very attractive due to her long, blond hair and athletic body type, but she rarely wore makeup or dressed up, preferring to focus on her cases, or just having a fun night out with her friends. Lillian, on the other hand, looked as if every inch of her body had been groomed impeccably. She had dark hair, that had been curled to perfection, and was sporting a perfect smokey eye and subtle pink lipstick. Her clothes were understated but expensive, a very chic little shift dress and a leather jacket. She seemed like the perfect Upper East Side socialite, somehow managing to be classic, and yet very cool and trendy at the same time. Mia wondered what kind of man would be brave enough to cheat on this woman.

"So," Mia asked. "What specifically can I do for you? I know you were having some issues with your boyfriend."

"Yes," Lillian replied. "He's been acting really shady recently. I have no idea what brought it on, but he's been coming home later and later every night, and he either lies or he just won't tell me where he's been. I'm pretty sure he's been cheating on me, but I want proof."

"I'm very sorry to hear that, Lillian. I'll get started on it right away. I was thinking maybe I could take a temp position at Will

Golden, that would allow me to get close to him and really see what he's been up to," said Mia.

"I would really appreciate that," Lillian said, a note of relief in her voice. "I'll pay you whatever you want, I just need to know the truth."

They quickly discussed payment, and Mia settled the check before they left. Mia wasn't sure how she felt about Lillian, but she found the idea of investigating Alexander Will very intriguing. Furthermore, she was sure it wouldn't be difficult to catch him cheating. Feeling optimistic, she decided to go see her friend, Lily before heading home for the night.

Lily Brooklyn was one of those people you couldn't help but love. She was a florist and owner of Lily's Flower Shop, and she had a very sweet and patient temperament. Mia liked the contrast between their personalities, because while Mia was independent and determined, Lily was quiet, calm, and reasonable. Whenever one of them had a problem, the other always seemed to know how to fix it, and when something good happened, the other was always there to celebrate it. They had been best friends for over five years, and now Lily was finally getting married to her longtime boyfriend, Patrick Carter. Lily had asked her to be a bridesmaid last week, and Mia couldn't wait to hear all the details of their upcoming nuptials.

Lily was busy arranging a bouquet of peonies when Mia arrived, her hair tousled from the wind outside. "Lily!" she exclaimed. "Those peonies can wait. I want to hear all about the wedding! I feel like we've barely had a chance to talk since you got engaged!"

"I know, right?" Lily replied. "Patrick and I are incredibly excited. Although with the flower business booming at the moment, I've barely had time to plan anything. We decided on a venue last night, but that's as far as we've gotten."

"That's still a progress," said Mia, grinning widely at her thoughtfully. "I'm just so happy Patrick finally proposed. It was a long time coming. You two are so perfect together."

"Thank you," Lily said, blushing. "But what about you? Are there any men in your life right now?" she added with a teasing voice.

"Not at the moment," Mia said. Many women would be embarrassed of admitting that, but not Mia. "I'm pretty satisfied with my career right now. I just got a new case that's going to keep me occupied for a little bit."

"But don't you ever want to settle down?" Lily asked. She always had been a hopeless romantic. "Or get married? I know you love being independent, but there has to be someone out there for you."

"Maybe eventually," Mia replied. "But I'm pretty contented right now. I feel like it will happen when it happens, you know?"

"I guess you're right," Lily said with a sigh. "I just would be happy to see you fall in love, for a change."

***

Chapter 2

Mia woke up bright and early the next morning, ready for the challenge of starting her investigation into Alexander Will. She dressed in subdued, professional outfit--- grey pencil skirt and navy blouse, and tied her hair back into a neat chignon. Her plan was to go to the Will Golden Corporation headquarters downtown and see if there were any open positions she could apply for.

Mia got off the train about two hours later and looked up at the skyscraper where Will Golden was housed. It was huge, and would have been quite intimidating. Had she been actually serious about a career there? She squared off her shoulders and walked in, heading for the reception desk.

"Hi!," she said brightly, addressing the young woman at the front desk. "I just wanted to inquire about any open positions you may have."

"As a matter of fact, we actually did just have a job open up," the receptionist replied. "Jayden Steele's secretary just quit a few days ago. We still haven't found a replacement. Is that something you might be interested in?"

Jayden Steele was the vice president of the company, as Mia had found out last night when she was doing some research to prepare for the case. She had no idea she'd have the opportunity to work for someone with such a high ranking in the company!

"I'd love to apply," Mia said. "How do I do that?"

"I'll set up an interview for you right now, and you can fax your resume over to us later. What's your name?" the receptionist asked.

"Umm... Sarah. Sarah... Shaw," Mia said.

Jayden Steele's office, predictably, was huge, located on one of the corners of the twentieth floor, and had full floor to ceiling windows on two sides. It was minimally decorated, and outfitted with a sleek grey computer and ergonomic chairs. Mia was peacefully reclining in one of the chairs when Jayden burst through the door. She sat up immediately and assumed her best, most professional posture. Jayden was tall and blonde, sort of Scandinavian looking, with a friendly, boyish air about him. Mia relaxed as she realized that he wasn't the slightest bit intimidating.

"Hi, you're Sarah, correct?" he asked. "I'm Jayden Steele. I just want to get to know a little bit about you before we can hire you officially. Honestly, I'm completely desperate for a secretary right now. Four days of trying to work without one has left me completely swamped. As long as you're relatively competent and polite, I'm sure we'll work well together."

Mia laughed a bit, starting to loosen up. This was going to be the easiest piece of detective work ever. "It's nice to meet you, Mr. Steele. My name's Sarah Shaw. I have my bachelor's degree in business from UCLA, and I moved to New York a few years ago and have been doing secretarial work ever since. I like to think I'm pretty organized and efficient, and can work well with a wide variety of people."

None of this is even really a lie, Mia thought. *There's no harm in using a different name.*

"Well, that sounds great, Sarah! I'm just going to ask you a few more questions, and you'll be officially hired. In fact, I really need you to come take minutes at our board meeting this afternoon. Are you up for that?" Jayden asked enthusiastically.

"Of course," Mia replied with a smile. She'd have to remember to start responding to the name Sarah from now on.

The board meeting was to be held in a very large conference room on the top floor of the building. Mia sat in a chair in the corner away from the table with a laptop, ready to record the minutes of the meeting. The room was starting to fill up, and people were slowly finding their places at the table. Mia looked up from her computer to see Jayden walking towards her.

"Just do your best, okay?" he said. "I know we sort of threw you in here, but even if you don't get everything right on the first try, it's better than me not having a secretary at all."

"Okay, thank you, Mr. Steele," Mia said with a smile.

"Please, call me Jayden," he replied with a wink.

Then the door opened, and a very tall man with dark brown hair and an arrogant swagger about him entered the room. Mia correctly assumed that this was the infamous Alexander Will.

"Okay, everyone, what have we got going on today? I want to hear all of your ideas about how we can improve this company's performance," Alexander said.

He had a deep voice and an extremely confident air about him. Mia got the impression that he could have been talking about something completely insignificant and the entire room still would have listened, completely captivated.

Mia continued to take notes on everything said in the meeting for the next hour, until finally everyone stood up to leave. She was packing up her laptop when she realized that none other than Alexander Will himself was standing right in front of her.

"Are you Jayden's new secretary? I haven't seen you here before," Alexander said.

"Yes, my name is.. Sarah Shaw," Mia replied, momentarily forgetting her alias. Alexander may have been a womanizer, but he was still one of the most attractive men she'd ever met. "It's nice to officially meet you, Mr. Will."

"Call me Xander. I'm sure we'll have a great time working together," he replied. Mia held out her hand for a handshake, but instead Xander raised it to his lips and kissed it. He then winked at her and walked out the door.

What a sleazeball, Mia thought. *He's known me for all of sixty seconds and he's already flirting with me.* If she hadn't felt bad for Lillian before, she most certainly did now.

***

Chapter 3

With a little ingenuity, Mia was able to gather all of the evidence she needed to prove that Xander was, in fact, guilty of cheating on Lillian. She chatted with the other secretaries about him, using the microphone on her cell phone to record everything they said. They told her salacious stories of all the women he was supposedly seeing behind Lillian's back, about his history of cheating on his girlfriends, and about his love of alcohol and drunken hookups. Armed with this evidence, Mia decided to sneak into Xander's office when he was on his lunch, and see what information she could get off of his computer.

Mia had done a computer science minor in college, and she had enough knowledge to be able to hack into Xander's computer as long as he didn't have an encrypted password. Luckily, Xander didn't have much in the way of security on his personal laptop, which he was silly enough to leave in an unlocked desk drawer. She quickly found flirty emails and instant messages with girls that clearly weren't Lillian, which she forwarded to herself, so she could print them out later. In one of the messages, he had discussed getting drinks at a bar across the town tonight with one of the girls. Mia decided to tail him so she could get some pictures, figuring it would be the final nail in the coffin of Xander and Lillian's relationship.

The next morning, she summoned Lillian to the Hudson Diner again, so she could show her the evidence she had compiled. She had the photos and emails printed out and organized in a file, and she also had an MP3 of the secretaries gossiping on a flash drive. Mia sat drinking coffee for twenty minutes, the file sitting on the table in front of her, before Lillian showed up. She looked disheveled, like she'd been crying for hours, and she was wearing a big sweater and leggings instead of the chic designer clothing she'd worn for their last meeting.

"Is everything okay?" Mia asked as Lillian sat down. "I don't mean to pry, but you seem really upset."

"Xander dumped me last night. Turns out I didn't even need all this evidence you got for me. He doesn't even feel guilty. He wants to 'play the field', apparently. His words, not mine," Lillian said with a sob.

"I'm incredibly sorry to hear that," Mia said. "Let me buy you some breakfast. I'm sure you could use some hot coffee and a big stack of pancakes. You can just cry if you need to." Mia was used to jilted girlfriends crying to her after she'd discovered less than savory things about their boyfriends or husbands, and she was an expert in making them feel better. "And of course, this file is yours to keep. You never know when you may need this information."

"Thank you so much, Mia," said Lillian. "I knew he wasn't the best boyfriend or anything, but I never thought he would actually dump me. We've been together for four years, you know. Our families are friends now, and we share a lot of the same friends... I just don't know what I'll do without him. We were always kind of a power couple, you know, because we're both quite social, and invested in our careers. How am I going to face everything by myself?"

"I know it seems dire now, Lillian, but you're a very strong woman," Mia said. "You really don't need him to be happy, or successful. And anyway, he treated you horribly. He doesn't deserve you at all."

"I actually was thinking about that," Lillian said. "I want him to feel, just once, how much this hurts, how I feel right now. And I have a request for you."

"What is it?" Mia asked.

"This is going to sound crazy," Lillian said with an angry glint in her eye. "But what if you seduced him? And then broke his heart? It would be easy enough. You're already working there, and he has a thing for secretaries. Especially pretty blonde ones. He'd never see it coming. And then maybe after this he would know better than to mess with me, or any of his girlfriends."

Mia was completely taken aback. How would she seduce Xander? He was one of the wealthiest men in the country, maybe even in the world. Surely, he had higher standards than her? And that was besides the fact that it was completely wrong. Xander may be a horrible person, but she didn't want to get involved with something this malicious.

"Lillian, I know you're angry right now, and I'm sure he deserves it, but I just can't do that," she said. "You're going to have to find someone else to seduce him."

"I'm sorry to hear that," Lillian said, full of disappointment all over her face. But still, she's hopeful. "Please let me know if you change your mind. I just can't stand to see him get away with this."

***

Mia was walking back towards her apartment when she passed an elegant hotel with several limousines parked outside. It was raining hard, and she decided to stop under the hotel's awning and dry off for a minute before resuming her trek home.

Mia started looking at the limousines and the people getting in and out of them. There were elegant older ladies dressed in Chanel, dapper businessmen in suits, and sexy young socialites and models in trendy little dresses and jackets. Most of their drivers stopped and walked them to the door of the hotel, holding an umbrella so they wouldn't get wet.

Mia wondered what it would be like to be one of these people, living their charmed lives. She'd had to work so hard for everything she had in her life. She'd paid her entire way through college on a part-time retail job and some loans when her parents split up and couldn't afford it. Every serious relationship she'd ever been in had ended terribly. She'd worked soul crushing entry level jobs for years before finally starting her own private investigation service. She was finally starting to feel like she was getting somewhere in life after years of toughing it out.

She felt so far away from these sparkling, beautiful people, even though they were standing right next to her.

Suddenly, something caught her eye in one of the limos. It looked like a young couple going at it in the backseat. Appalled, Mia walked a little closer, with a sense of morbid curiosity.

"They couldn't at least wait until they got into the hotel?" she thought.

Then, she realized something --- the silhouette of the man in the car looked an awful lot like Xander Will. In fact, she was pretty sure it was Xander Will, messing around with some model who clearly wasn't Lillian Davis.

Feeling a sense of frustration at the entire male gender in general, Mia pulled out her phone and called Lillian. "I'll do it," she said.

"What?" Lillian said. She still sounded like she had been crying.

"I'll help you with your little revenge plot. You're right. He can't get away with this."

***

Chapter 4

Jayden walked into the office the next morning looking extremely chipper. He tossed an embossed card on 'Sarah's' desk as he passed by.

"I hope you clean up nice, new girl," he said. "Because you're coming with me to this party on Friday night."

Mia looked at the invitation. It informed her that she was now invited to attend a party at a five-star hotel uptown that was celebrating the work of a few high-profile charities. Many of the Will Golden employees would be there, as well as successful employees from other Fortune 500 companies throughout the city.

Xander will probably be there, Mia thought. *This will be the perfect opportunity to put Lillian's plan in motion.*

***

Lillian had generously offered to take Mia on shopping before the party to help her find the perfect dress. She also had offered up the services of her hair and makeup team, which she had on retainer to prep her for all of her events as heir to Davis Mining Company.

"After spending so much time with him, I know exactly what he likes," she told Mia. "There's no way you won't catch his eye tonight."

After a few hours of trying on dresses that weren't quite right, they finally found the perfect dress: a midnight blue, floor length Marchesa. It had an open back, which Lillian claimed Xander would love, and beautiful floral detailing on the front. The hairstylist then put Mia's normally straight hair into beautiful, loose curls, and the makeup artist gave Mia the perfect smokey eye.

Mia stood up and looked at herself in the full length mirror, doing a slow twirl. She had never gotten this dressed up for anything in her life, and she liked the way she felt. She felt like a princess, or maybe a model.

"Thank you, Lillian," she said enthusiastically. "You've been so generous. I won't let you down."

"Just make sure the bastard gets what has coming to him," Lillian growled in reply. "You do look amazing, though. There's no way this won't work."

Mia stepped out of the limousine, momentarily starstruck. All around her, there were beautiful, well-known people in black tie suits and floor length dresses. She forgot for a second that she was supposed to be one of them tonight. And she was also late to meet Jayden, who had wanted to talk to her before the party started, as it was technically a work function for her.

She saw him waiting on the steps outside the entrance, answering emails on his phone. *He looked very nice in his suit*, Mia thought. She ran up the steps as fast as her dress would permit. "Sorry I'm a little late!" she said. "The hair and makeup took longer than I thought they would."

"No worries, Sarah," Jayden said. "You look absolutely radiant. I'm so glad to have you here. I really want you to enjoy yourself tonight. I just need you to come check in with me every once in a while. I may need to add things to my calendar or make a quick note, and as my secretary, you handle all of that stuff. But it should be a mainly social event."

"Sounds good. I'll be honest, Jayden, I've never been to something like this before. It's quite intimidating."

"Don't worry," Jayden said. "I'll help you through it. These people seem intimidating, but really, they are just like everyone else. They have their own insecurities and problems. You'll see."

And with that, he offered her his arm, which Mia took as they strode into the party.

Inside was rather dark, with mood lighting everywhere creating a soft glow. There were numbered tables and a small open area with a little podium, where people were currently mingling and where, Mia assumed, there would later be speeches. Everyone was currently mingling, and as they walked in, heads slowly turned to look at them.

"I'm glad I have you on my arm tonight," Jayden whispered in Mia's ear. "You may be new at this, but you're already turning heads."

They walked around for a while, chatting with various important business people. Jayden introduced Mia to everyone, and she was surprised at how friendly and fun he was. They were seated together at dinner, where they continued to chat. Mia was engaged in the conversation, but she kept looking around, trying to find Xander. Finally, she found him two tables over, and accidentally made eye contact. She looked away immediately, turning her focus to Jayden and smiling. But when she looked back a few minutes later, Xander was still looking at her, an intense expression on his face.

Just then, the hosts of the party stood up to make speeches about the charities that were being sponsored that night. Then, they invited everyone to dance. Jayden turned to Mia and held out his hand. She accepted, and he lead her to the dance floor, where he pulled her into a slow waltz. Jayden was a skilled dancer, and soon they were whirling around the dance floor, the other couples just a blur of flowing silk and black suits.

"This is fun," Mia said. "I've never been a good dancer, but you make it feel easy."

"Thank you," Jayden said. "I was forced into cotillion when I was young. I guess that's where I learned everything."

They continued to chat amicably until Mia felt a firm hand on her shoulder. She turned around to find herself looking straight into Xander Will's deep brown eyes.

"Sorry, Jay, d'you mind if I cut in?" he said, his eyes still on Mia. "Your date's the belle of the ball tonight. I didn't want to miss out on a chance to dance with her."

"Whatever you want, boss," Jayden said irritably.

"So," Xander said with a flirtatious glint in his eye. "Tell me something about yourself, Sarah. You look absolutely stunning tonight, but you seem so.. *mysterious*."

"Well, Mr. Will, that's probably because I'm not one of those secretaries that follows you around like a lost puppy, hoping you'll pet me."

"My secretaries do not do that!" Xander replied indignantly.

"They most certainly do. But that's alright. I can't say I blame them. I just wish they had a little more dignity. But anyway... Something about myself? I'm really not that interesting... I grew up in California, went to business school in Los Angeles, and then moved here when I was twenty-one, hoping to live out my dreams in New York City, thinking it would be life changing. But mostly I've just been doing boring secretarial work."

"Surely you're capable of more than that.. You seem intelligent, Sarah, and you're charming and beautiful on top of it. What were those dreams you came here to pursue?"

"I don't know.. I just wanted to be the one running the meetings, instead of taking notes at them, or grabbing the bosses' coffee. I think I could do more than just answer phones and type, you know? Or actually, you probably don't. You've never been a secretary. I'm so sorry, I didn't mean to complain to you. I should be thankful I have any job at all, and you just wanted to have a fun night."

Xander put a finger to her lips in a playful way, and Mia was surprised at the intimacy of the gesture. "It's all right," he said. "Just dance with me. I know how it feels to be constantly working, never feeling like you're getting where you want to go... I know it doesn't seem like it, but I've had to work very hard to get where I am, and to stay there. Just relax and enjoy being the most beautiful girl in the room."

The party was starting to clear out, but Mia and Xander were still dancing. A friend of Xander's came over and gently tapped him on the shoulder. "Just so you know, it's almost one in the morning," he said. "I think they are going to want everyone to clear out of here soon."

"I guess that's my cue to leave," Mia said.

"Wait," Xander replied. "Can I at least get your phone number? I love talking to you. You're… easy to be around. I don't have many people like that in my life."

The pair pulled out their smartphones and quickly traded numbers. "Where do you live?" Xander asked.

"Downtown, about twenty blocks south of here."

"Damn, I'm headed in the opposite direction, otherwise I'd offer to take you home. I'll call you a car, though."

Mia watched as the city lights flew by outside the window of her town car. She was feeling tired from all the dancing, and had to force herself to keep her eyes open. No matter how long she lived here, she would never get used to the beauty of the twinkling skyline at night, and she always tried to absorb it all.

Lillian had been right, it had been incredibly easy to get Xander interested in her. She'd barely even had to do anything, other than make eye contact and respond when he talked to her. She was surprised, though; he'd been nicer to her than she'd anticipated. She still thought he was a horrible womanizer, after all, he'd just barely broken up with Lillian and he was already trying to flirt with her. But she was starting to understand why women were so charmed by him.

Her phone buzzed, and she looked down to see that Xander was calling her.

"*Already?*" she thought.

But she figured she might as well answer, the sooner she truly seduced him, the sooner she could break his heart and be done with this case.

She picked up the phone. "Hello?"

"Hi, Sarah," he said. "I know this may seem... soon. And very impulsive. But I have a request for you."

"What is it?" Mia asked, slightly bewildered.

"Would you want to come out of town with me this weekend? My girl--- *er*, the person I planned the trip with, uh, she canceled on me. And I would really like to get to know you better. Please say yes."

"That sounds wonderful, Xander. Yes, I would love to spend the weekend with you."

***

Chapter 5

Xander had decided to take her out to the Hamptons for a weekend, and a car pulled up in front of her apartment around nine in the morning. The chauffer stepped out and opened the door for her, and Mia stepped in, not totally sure what to expect.

Xander was sitting in the back, looking much more relaxed than usual in chinos and a polo instead of his usual work suit. He held out a piping hot coffee and a bag containing a blueberry scone. "I got you some breakfast for the road," he said. "I hope you like caramel macchiatos. I didn't know what coffee you usually drink so I figured that was a safe bet."

"Thank you," Mia said. She decided that there were definitely worse things in the world than seducing beautiful, rich men who brought her breakfast. "So what are we doing today?"

"I thought I would take you to my favorite beach in Southampton. It has one of the most beautiful ocean views you've ever seen. I know you're from California and everything, but we have some pretty incredible coastline here, too."

Mia laughed. "I'll believe that when I see it," she said. "I grew up going to Newport Beach on the weekends. That will be pretty hard to beat. But that does sounds fun."

Xander had been right, the beach was amazing. There were miles of beautiful white sand, and lucky for them, there wasn't a cloud in the sky. "I stand corrected," Mia said. "This is really wonderful."

Xander gave her a playful little shove. "See, I told you," he said. "And I have a surprise for you." He pulled two bottles of top-notch white wine and a picnic basket from the back of the car. "I thought this might be more fun than going out to lunch. I had my personal chef at home make us some sandwiches, and I think there are fresh strawberries in there as well."

"Do you do this for all the girls, or is it just me?" Mia asked jokingly. Xander's face fell.

"I wasn't going to tell you this, but I actually just broke up with my girlfriend," he said.

Mia tried to force her face into a surprised expression. "I'm so sorry to hear that," she said, keeping her voice high and girlish in hopes that it would sound sympathetic. "I had no idea."

"Yeah," he said. "It was a long time coming, I guess. I was pretty horrible to her, always flirting with other girls and stuff. But we fell out of love a while ago. There was no spark there anymore. It just wasn't worth it."

"Well," Mia said, flirtatiously, "Let's drink to new beginnings, then." She grabbed the bottles of wine and ran down towards the beach, her long hair streaming behind her in the sea breeze. Xander stood there for a moment, appreciating the view, and then ran after her.

Two hours and several glasses of wine later, Mia and Xander were feeling uninhibited, to say the least. In fact, they had been getting along wonderfully. Xander was surprisingly funny, and he had a sarcastic side that Mia had not anticipated at all. "So, are you enjoying your day out?" he asked her.

"I actually really am," Mia said, actually meaning it. She was starting to feel bad for what she was going to do to him. But then, she remembered Lillian, and how upset she had been, and decided it was justified.

"I'm so glad you're here. This may sound strange, but you're the first person in a long time that I feel like I can truly relax with. When I'm in the city, I feel like I'm always trying, you know? Like I have to live up to what everyone expects me to be," Xander said.

"But you always seem so confident. That's what everyone loves about you - it seems like you're *not* trying."

"That couldn't be farther from the truth. I inherited this company at twenty when my dad passed away - I had no idea what I was doing. I was far too young to be running a business, especially one this big and this important. I didn't have anyone to guide me at all, and at the time I was actually pretty shy. It was sink or swim, and I decided losing myself was okay if it meant I was still swimming."

"Wow, I didn't realize that. It just always seemed like everything came really naturally to you."

"Not at all. I sacrificed a lot of things that were important to me in order to be successful. I used to have a lot of friends--- real ones, not people that I pretend to be friends with for professional reasons, or girls I just hook up with. Somewhere along the way I lost all that. It's amazing how you can be surrounded by people all the time and still be lonely, you know?"

"I do. I can actually really relate to that," Mia said. This was bad. Now she was starting to feel sorry for him. *Snap out of it, Mia,* she thought. *He just wants to sleep with you. There's no way any of this stuff is true.* But she wasn't sure how much she even believed that.

The sun was starting to set by now, and the beach was starting to clear off. "Hey," Mia said, putting her hand on Xander's arm. "Why don't we go get another drink."

They found themselves in a dark, smoky pub, full of rowdy townies and college kids dancing and playing pool. "This is totally not a place I would expect you to go," Mia said as Xander grabbed them some vodka shots from the bartender.

"This is the best kind of bar," Xander said. "Everyone's just here to have a good time. Also, no one knows or cares that I'm the CEO of Will Golden, so that's a plus."

"Except me, of course," Mia said with a wink. "I hope you trust me with your secret."

"You, and no one else," Xander said.

He sat down at a booth in the corner of the bar, and grabbed her waist and pulled her to him. All of a sudden, Mia was very aware of how close they were, and his arm around her. She wondered what it would be like to kiss him, but shook the thought out of her head. *Don't get too involved with this*, she thought. *You're just doing this for Lillian. That's all.*

Xander grabbed his shot and raised it for a toast. "Oh god," Mia said. "I haven't done shots since college. What are we drinking to?"

"Us," Xander said, and they downed their shots as quickly as they could.

"That was terrible," Mia said, shaking her head. "There's a reason usually stick with wine."

"But don't you feel so much better now?"

"You know, I kind of do." And it was true. Mia was starting to feel the warmth moving through her body, her muscles loosening up. "You're a terrible influence, Mr. Will."

"Oh, you don't know the half of it," he said with a grin. "Why don't we head back to the hotel, and I'll show you just how bad of an influence I can be."

Mia knew she should be appalled by the cheesy line, and that going back to the hotel was a terrible idea, but she was starting to feel really drunk, and she was really intrigued by Xander.

"Okay," she said. "Let's go. Before you get me even more drunk."

They wandered through the streets of the Southampton, laughing as they held on to each other for balance. Finally, they reached the hotel, a tasteful old inn that was a favorite of wealthy Manhattanites on vacation. Xander had booked them a large corner suite on the top floor, with a big bay window facing the beach.

They fell on the bed almost as soon as they were in the door. Xander kissed her deeply, and instead of resisting like she knew she should, Mia kissed him back. After that, things started to blur together, and before Mia knew it, they were having sex, and she was enjoying it way more than she'd ever intended to.

"You were very hard to get than I thought," he whispered to him, trying to seduce her even more.

"Am I really?" she asked, amused. Mia wasn't able to resist him anymore. She wanted the way Alexander Will feasts on her body. Surprisingly, the trace of Lillian's memory vanished at the moment.

Naked and hungry for each other, both of them savored the gratifying sensation of what they could possibly call a one-night stand.

"*Oh, Xander,*" she gasped submissively as he started to dig deeper, and thrust majestically to feel her. "This is... We shouldn't..."

He kissed her roughly, to stop her from protesting. Alexander stares at her with deep, seducing eyes, and she knew by then that she was already captivated by him. He continued to push himself inside of her, trying to weigh how far he could go. *Ohh...* she thought.

Alexander's hand travels around her skin, cupping her full breasts greedily. "Damn, Sarah," he said, appreciatively. "You're trying to cross my line, but I like it," he continued, then softly sucks one of her nipples, while going deeper and deeper.

Sarah's body burns madly. This is all wrong, but she just can't help it. He is too gorgeous, too beautiful, and divine. Soon enough, she found herself voluntarily following his rhythm, unable to control her aching body anymore.

"Fuck!" he howled in gratification. *"Oh Sarah..."* he whispered, gritting his teeth.

She smiled at him pleasantly, full of desires and thirst. Abruptly, Alexander went back to own her lips, invading her mouth possessively and biting her neck at a time. When Mia closed her eyes, she felt him freeing himself, his lips going down to her sex. *Oh, no! He wouldn't---?* She breathed in panic, but the sensation of his soft tongue eventually soothes her aching piece.

"Oh, Damn! This is crazy!" she let out, squirming at his sweet torture.

She found him staring at her with a mischievous, satisfied grin. Slowly, he eases one of his fingers inside and teases her clitoris. "Oh, baby. You're even more beautiful when you're wet," he whispered, watching her while she glory in pleasure.

"I-I can't hold it any longer," she panted, her legs feeling numb and rigid.

She clasped the pillow above her, and scratched Xander's back with her other hand. He knew she is finally meeting her orgasm, so, abruptly, he guided himself inside her sex once more, and continuously pushed his enormous muscle without any mercy. His eyes were dark, and dangerous, yet quite engrossing to look at.

"AH! Xander! Oh, don't stop!" Sarah whimpered, completely exploding and releasing her climax. She felt the sweet, sweet secretion of her delicate piece, and finally, she lost all the strength to keep up with his pace.

It didn't take long when the lovely man found his release too. She called out her name, and collapses on top of her in a complete satisfaction and wonder.

Mia lay in bed after it was over and Xander had passed out, knowing she should feel guilty, but she couldn't bring herself to feel anything other than exhaustion. She slowly passed out into a drunken slumber.

Chapter 6

"Wake up, sleepyhead. I ordered room service," Xander said, opening the curtains.

"Ughhh, it's too bright. And too loud," Mia said. Her head was throbbing from all the alcohol. She sat up slowly, and opened her eyes to a massive buffet on a tray table next to her. There were scrambled eggs, fresh orange juice, and big, fluffy pancakes.

"I hope you like it," Xander said, looking uncharacteristically nervous.

"Of course I like it!" Mia said. "This is the perfect hangover cure. That's very sweet of you, Xander. Thank you."

"I went and talked to the chef downstairs and asked him to make you the perfect Sunday morning breakfast. He's done some of the food for Will Golden events in the past. He's really very good."

"Wait," Mia said. "How are you not in a hungover!? How did you have the energy to get up and talk to the chef? I don't think we even fell asleep until after two last night."

"Well, you were too drunk to realize, but I was drinking water in between the wine and the shots. I assumed you were doing the same, but clearly I was wrong."

"It's been a long time since I've been that drunk. Clearly, my partying skills are a little rusty."

Xander laughed at her, though not unkindly. "Come on, eat your breakfast and get dressed. I have another surprise for you this afternoon."

Mia was starting to wonder if she should go through with Lillian's plan. Sure, Xander had done some horrible things, but he also seemed like he was incredibly lonely and sad, and she didn't want to make that worse. Plus, he was treating her like a princess and she couldn't remember the last time any man had done that for her.

Xander's surprise turned out to be that he actually owned a small island off the coast of Southampton. They walked over to a pier from the hotel, where Xander had chartered a boat to take them over to see it.

"I wasn't even going to show you this originally, because I think it kind of makes me seem like a pompous asshole. But my family's owned this island for generations. My great-grandfather built a little beach house over here almost a hundred years ago, and the land's just been passed down through the family. It's my favorite place in the world," he said.

The boat ride took about twenty minutes, and if the breakfast hadn't cured Mia's hangover, this certainly did. The wind blew through Mia's hair and hit her in the face, making her feel strangely alive in a way that was rare for her. They got off the boat and found themselves on a small beach surrounded by trees. There was a path up off of the beach that lead to a small, but charming little house.

"Come inside," Xander said. "I want to show you around."

The house was just as inviting on the inside as it was on the outside. There was a cute little living room with cozy couches and family photos hanging on the wall. Directly across from that, there was a small kitchen with pale yellow tiling. There was a small spiral staircase that led directly above them to a second floor.

"Come on," Xander said, taking Mia's hand, and gently leading her up the stairs. "I want to show you the bedroom."

They sat down on a large bed in a room with sloping ceilings and floral decor. "So," Xander said. "Last night was pretty incredible."

"I had a lot of fun," Mia said. "But I'm not sure it was the best idea. I mean, you're my boss. I feel like that's probably breaking some sort of rule." Better to break it off now, she thought, than make the situation any more complicated than it needs to be.

But then, Xander grabbed her waist and pulled her towards him.

"How could this be wrong? This feels more right to me than anything I've done in a long time," he murmured, sweetly.

He kissed her, more softly, romantically, than he had before. And Mia decided to stop resisting. She started to kiss him back, and let her hand traveled on his firm muscles. Both of them grinned as she stopped on the bulging piece in between his thigh.

"See how it wants you?" Xander uttered in a very alluring way. Immediately, he pinned her to the wall as he peeled off her clothes.

"Please, let me touch you now, Sarah. I want you to make love to me without the alcohol's influence," he pleaded.

"O-okay," she breathed weakly, and soon enough, Alexander's skillful hand was wandering all over her body again.

"Crazy, isn't it? I don't know what you've done to me. You are completely bewitching me, Sarah," he said, and bit her earlobe softly. This sends a strange sensation to her. Suddenly, she wanted to please him.

Cautiously, Mia maneuvered him, and pressed him on the wall instead. She got on her knees, and pulled down his shorts. Alexander gazed at her in anticipation as she grasped her sized. Then, she sheeted her teeth with her lips and put him in her mouth.

"Ah, baby," he grumbled, appreciatively. "You have no idea what you're doing to me," he uttered, clutching her hair to get a better view.

Though a bit inexperienced when it comes to this part, Mia was satisfied to see him howling with pleasure. For her, he wasn't the typical CEO of the company, but an ordinary man, who sincerely wanted to make love to her. She continued to please him, pushing him deep down her throat.

"Argh!" Xander grunted wildly. "Come here," he said, and pulled her up. He shifted her swiftly on the bed, then spreads her legs apart. Then, he kneeled down beside the mattress, and licked her sweet and soft private part. "Beautiful," he whispered appreciatively.

Mia squirmed as he inserts his tongue skillfully inside her. All the blood in her veins runs wildly, as if he is sending out some fire to boil them.

"Hmm.." Alexander said, maliciously. "Now, tell me it wasn't right, honey. I am willing to stop," he teased her.

Mia knew she couldn't afford to let him stop from whatever he was doing right now. She completely burnt in glorious pain, and aching madly for his wonderful assault once again.

"No," she protested. "Do whatever you wish to my body, Xander," she urged him, guiding his hand to touch her breasts.

"Damn, it's my pleasure to do that," he replied, climbing hungrily on top of her.

Mia spreads her legs more to give him an easier access, and eagerly, he sinks his penis deliciously inside her.

"*Oh...*" Mia gasped, willingly accepting his intrusion.

"You're so wet already," he commented, smooching her neck while caressing her nipples. "Looks like you do want me too," he smiled.

"Yes... I want you..." she admitted helplessly.

And as if it's his cue, Xander started to thrust greedily, pushing himself in and out of Mia's perilously addicting flower. The bed's distracting screeching sounds spiced up their hunger for each other.

"I want to take you from behind," Xander said in a firm tone after a while. "Turn around," he ordered, and Mia obeyed him readily.

In no time, Xander was hitting on her once again. Mia was surprised to feel his fullness even more. She never thought that this position can actually give her more pleasure.

"Oh!" she cried in sweet agony. She pushes her hips harder to match with his speed.

"Damn, baby," Xander growled, squeezing both the cheeks of her behind. "You seem to enjoy this as much as I do," he commented again as he dig deeper and tougher.

"Yes…" she panted. "Hit me harder," she requested.

Then, Mia moaned unexpectedly as he smashed her delicious spot, which made her legs tremble hysterically. They both knew that both of them are coming closer, so without any hesitations, they boosted their speed to gratify each other's senses.

Alexander and Mia called out each other's name as they burst into extreme climax, and with one final blow, they exchanged the fruit of their sweet orgasms and fell down, panting and gasping for breath.

Two hours later, Mia rolled over and gently touched Xander's shoulder, waking him up from his nap. "We should probably head back to the city soon," she said.

"*Ugh*," he groaned. "Back to reality." He sat up slowly. Mia admired his abs, and his nice strong arms. She wondered when he ever found the time to work out. They both got up and slowly started to dress and pack up their things. "I'll call the boat, and I'll have my driver meet us at the dock in Southampton."

Mia wondered if she would ever have a romantic weekend this perfect again. She went over to Xander, and reached up and kissed him on the cheek.

"Thank you," she said. Then, she picked up her bag and headed down the stairs and out to meet the boat.

***

Chapter 7

When they were sitting in the car on their way back into the city, Xander was uncharacteristically quiet. He just took her hand and smiled.

After twenty minutes of companionable silence, Mia said, "I'm so sad that this weekend had to end. I could not have imagined anything better."

"Maybe it doesn't have to…" Xander said after a while, looking rather mischievous.

"What do you have in mind?"

"Hey, can you get off on the next exit? And pull into the motel right off the highway."

Mia laughed. "You're not serious!"

"Sarah, I am as serious as I've ever been in my entire life," he said, but he couldn't contain his smile.

They got to the motel and checked into the first available room. Xander pressed her up against the door as soon as it was shut, kissing her with an aggressiveness Mia hadn't yet seen in him. He started unbuttoning her shirt, and she pushed him back onto the bed.

"If this is the last time…" she said, uncertainly.

"It won't be," he replied. "But if it is, we better make it good, then."

***

Mia woke up sometime later that evening, noticing that it was pouring rain outside. She decided that when she got back to the city, she would call Lillian and cancel the revenge plan. It wasn't fair to Xander, or to her. She didn't want to break his heart, no matter what horrible things he'd done in the past. After all, it wasn't like she'd never made a mistake in her life, and she certainly wouldn't like to be punished in the way that Lillian wanted her to punish Xander. She also thought it might be a good idea for her to resign from her job. Even if Xander thought it wouldn't be a problem, she was sure that sleeping with the boss might get her in trouble with Jayden. She also didn't want to be the subject of office gossip. She wanted the connection between her and Xander to be something that stayed private and special, just for them to enjoy.

No matter how much she tried to deny it to herself, she was completely falling head over heels for Xander.

She sat up and started looking for her clothes, but then she noticed that Xander was already dressed, with a very somber look on his face. "I think maybe you were right after all. This wasn't a good idea," he said.

"Wait, Xander, where is this coming from?" Mia's stomach dropped. How could this be happening? What had changed? "I know this won't be easy, but we'll work it out. I'll resign from Will Golden. I want to be with you. This weekend was so amazing. We can't give up this easily!"

"Yes, we can," Xander said, his eyes devoid of any emotion. He wasn't making eye contact with her either, but rather looking past her out the window at the pouring rain. "In fact, I've written you a check for your service. Thank you for your... company this weekend."

Mia noticed that there was a check for $25,000 on the nightstand next to her. "I hope you'll be discreet about this whole affair," Xander said. "I like to keep these things private." Mia stood up in an outrage. "Are you kidding me!? I don't need your money! I thought you were genuinely interested in me and wanted to be with me. What about all of that stuff you said about me being one of the few people you could open up to? It really didn't seem like you were making all of that up."

"You were just what I wanted this weekend. I would really prefer it if you would just take the payment, as a thank you from me, and we'll keep everything between us. I really shouldn't be sleeping with secretaries, anyway."

"Fine," Mia said. "I'll leave. And I'll stay quiet. But I'm not taking your money. I'm not some sort of prostitute," she hissed. "I deserve to be treated better than that."

She put her dress back on, and grabbed all of her things, and without another word, or a glance back at Xander, she walked straight out of the motel.

"Where's the nearest bus station?" she asked the concierge. A cab back to Manhattan from here would be way too expensive. She would wait for hours in the pouring rain if she had to.

***

Chapter 8

Mia woke up the next morning feeling completely exhausted. She had waited forty five minutes in the rain for the bus, and then the bus ride itself had taken almost three hours. She had been crying the entire time, and the other passengers kept asking her if she was okay, and handing her tissues. When she got home, she was completely drained that she passed out right away.

She still hadn't resigned from her job at Will Golden, so she still had to go into the office. She decided to put on a brave face and tough it out for another week or two. She would feel bad leaving Jayden hanging after he'd searched so hard to find a new secretary. She put on her favorite blouse and pencil skirt, put her hair up in a bun, and went to catch the train.

When she got into the office, the first thing she noticed was that there was an enormous bouquet of flowers on her desk. In fact, it was so big it was covering up everything else on the desk, and you couldn't even see in the window to Jayden's office, which was right behind it.

Mia was so excited. *Xander must have had a change of heart after all,* she thought.

She was still angry with him, of course, but she knew he struggled with relationships, and decided immediately that she would give him a second chance. They would work everything out, she knew they could do it.

Mia's coworkers were crowding around her desk now, asking her who the flowers were from, and what the occasion was.

"I don't know," Mia said, trying to be coy. "Let's find out." She opened the card attached to the vase, expecting to see a heartfelt note from Xander, but instead they were from.. Jayden?

Sarah,

Please enjoy these flowers. I had an absolutely wonderful time with you at the party on Friday night. I would love to spend more time with you (outside the office!) again soon.

Yours,

Jayden.

Mia's anger towards Xander flared right back up again. She'd been so stupid to think that he would really want to apologize. Really, she'd been stupid for falling for him in the first place. She'd heard of everything that he'd done to Lillian. She should have known better.

Just then, Jayden came walking around the corner. "I hope you like your flowers, Sarah," he beamed at her.

Mia forced her face into a smile. "I love them! You are so sweet. Thank you very much."

Even more people started to gather around, wanting to catch a bit of the gossip. Why was Jayden so interested in his secretary? Mia then realized that Alexander was standing towards the back of the crowd, watching her like a hawk. She got a chill, and realized that she was sweating bullets.

"Sarah, I know this is very soon, and you are my secretary and everything," Jayden said. "But I had a lovely time dancing with you at the party on Friday night. You are such a wonderful, kind person, you are very fun to talk to, and of course, you are beautiful. I was wondering if you would come out on an official date with me. I would love for you to be my girlfriend. I can always find another secretary, but it's very difficult to find someone as wonderful as you to have in my personal life. Please say yes."

Mia was completely taken aback. She had not expected this at all. She had thought that Jayden was just being friendly to her because he was her boss, not because he was interested in her. But then again, he was fun, nice, easygoing, the complete opposite of Xander, and he was cute in that golden boy sort of way.

Everyone was staring at her now, and Jayden was starting to look worried. She was completely aware of Xander's eyes on her, scrutinizing her. She would have to make a decision right now.

"Yes," she said, not totally aware of what she was doing. "Yes, I would love to be your girlfriend." The entire room burst into animated conversation. She smiled at Jayden, then looked briefly over at Xander, who was walking away, and shaking his head in obvious remorse.

***

Chapter 9

The next day, Mia came into work feeling very pleased with herself. Dating Jayden was sure to make Xander extremely jealous, and right now, all she wanted was for him to feel as horrible as she had when he wrote her that check. She had gone out to a boring, but still pleasant dinner with Jayden last night. She had made sure that everyone had seen them leave the office together, so that word would get back to Xander that they were, in fact, going out.

When Mia sat down at her desk, she realized that there was a memo from Jayden saying that Xander had sent him on an emergency trip to meet with the European branch of their company in London. He would be back in a week, he said, and if she could just keep everything organized for him and answer all of his calls, that would be great.

Then, Xander's secretary came up to her desk. "Mr. Will would like to see you in his office at your earliest convenience, please," she said to Mia.

Mia's stomach dropped. She had not been expecting him to react so quickly. "Tell him I'll be there in a few minutes," she said.

She went to the bathroom and made sure her hair and makeup were perfect, and then walked over to Xander's office and knocked on the door.

"Come in, please," he said. She walked in and sat down in the chair in front of his desk. "What's this about, Alexander?" she asked.

"How could you humiliate me like that yesterday?" he growled. "Why would you go out of your way to publicly date Jayden?"

Mia was confused, but also perversely glad to see him so upset. "I thought you wanted me to stay out of your life," she said. "This isn't doing you any harm at all. Why are you so mad?"

"Because he doesn't deserve you," he said. He then got up, locked the door, and shut the blinds. He yanked Mia up by her wrist so she was standing, and aggressively kissed her, pushing her up against the desk. He started tugging at the zipper on her skirt, but she pushed his hand away.

"This isn't the time, or the place," she said.

"You're right," he said, breathing heavily. "Meet me downstairs at one o'clock this afternoon. I'll have a car waiting to take us somewhere better."

Mia knew she should say no, but she was so captivated by Xander. He was even more magnetic when he was angry. Plus, she knew this weekend hadn't been a lie. He had to have felt something for her.

"I'll see you at one," she said before walking out of the office.

Xander took her out of the city, north this time, to his country house in Westchester. It was a huge, three story colonial, and looked like a palace on the inside, decorated with white marble and gold. He took her up to the master bedroom, which consisted only of a massive four poster bed, a chandelier, and a dresser. Without speaking, he pinned her down on the bed.

"I know you want this," he said, roughly. "Don't pretend to be mad at me."

Mia kissed him, and gave into what he wanted. She let him strip her down and have his way with her, and instead of being scared, she found herself enjoying it. Despite everything, her heart was still telling her that there was more to Xander than his horrible actions. She couldn't forget the sad look in his eye when they were sitting on the beach, talking about how lonely and isolated he felt in his life. And of course, she couldn't forget how he'd made her breakfast. How he'd told her she was beautiful and kind, and easy to be around.

After they'd had sex, she turned over and asked him, "Why did you feel like you needed to pay me last time? You know I'm not some sort of prostitute. I would have kept it quiet. I still will."

"I was intimidated by you. You weren't like the other girls I've dated, who have no personality and just nod and smile. You can actually carry on a conversation. You have your own life, and your own goals. And that scared me. I wanted to feel in control. I still do. It's a fatal flaw of mine… it caused a lot of problems with my ex."

"I guess you're just not used to not getting everything your way all the time."

"No, I'm not. And even though you seemed happy with me at the time, I knew you had been having doubts about us being together. I couldn't let you act on those. So I decided to do something about it first."

"Xander, I really do care about you. But you've done some horrible things. You can't keep acting like this if you want any of this to work out."

"How am I supposed to be a perfect gentleman when you're dating Jayden?! The guy is a total dud. You deserve only the best. You deserve someone that's going to make you feel like royalty, who's exciting and powerful and important."

Mia was taken aback by his intensity. She'd never met anyone so self-important, but she'd also never met anyone who would go to such great lengths to have her. But she couldn't just let him win. That would be too easy. He needed to learn that he couldn't just go around breaking her heart.

"This may be true, but I'm still with Jayden. I already feel badly about everything we've done here. How am I supposed to explain this to him? I want to be with you Xander, I really do, but this isn't the right way. He is a good guy. This isn't fair."

"I don't care about him. Or his feelings. You're meant for me. It's as simple as that."

"How about a compromise? I'll wait until Jayden gets back in the country, and I will break up with him, letting him down easy. We won't tell anyone about us until it all blows over."

"I can live with that," Xander said. He grabbed her and pulled her into a kiss. "I just want you all to myself."

**

Epilogue

Xander and Mia drove back to the city the next day, feeling tired but contented. They planned to keep everything a secret, until Jayden got back and Mia could break up with him. She hadn't decided yet what she would tell him. She would probably use a cliché breakup line, something like 'it's not you, it's me,' or 'I'm just not that into you". She figured the less she told him, the better. He would find out about her and Xander in due time, and he was sure to be very upset.

Xander kissed Mia when they were still in the car, and promised to see each other later, when they both had some free time. Then, they got out and went about their usual tasks at work. Mia felt ecstatic. She hadn't felt this way about anyone in such a long time. Indeed, being in love was wonderful.

At lunchtime, she decided to walk over to Xander's office just to say hello before she went out, and bought her food. But when she got to the office, she noticed that there was a woman there. Although she couldn't hear what they were saying, she could tell that Xander was talking to her very intently and seriously. The woman had dark, wavy hair, and after looking at her for a few minutes, Mia realized that it was Lillian!

What is she doing here? Mia thought. *They broke up. This cannot be good.*

Mia knew that although Xander clearly felt very passionate about her, there was no way she could compete with Lillian. After all, Lillian was rich, gorgeous, smart, and had already been Xander's girlfriend for years. Worse, she knew that Lillian can actually blow everything about her true identity. What is she going to do?

***

The End

The Fallen Revenge 2

Billionaire Romance

By: Lisa Cartwright

☐ **Copyright 2015 by Lisa Cartwright - All rights reserved.**

In no way is it legal to reproduce, duplicate, or transmit any part of this document in either electronic means or in printed format. Recording of this publication is strictly prohibited and any storage of this document is not allowed unless with written permission from the publisher. All rights reserved.

Respective authors own all copyrights not held by the publisher.

Prologue

Mia Madison was standing in shock outside Xander Will's office. She had come over to ask if he wanted to be out for a quick lunch, even though they had said they would avoid each other at work.

She couldn't get the memories of the last few days out of her head, the way that he had kissed her, touched her. But now, there was another woman sitting across from his desk, and that woman was most definitely Lillian Davis, who had secretly employed Mia to get revenge on Xander after he broke up with her. However, things hadn't exactly gone according to plan.

Before Mia could decide whether to knock and figure out what was going on, or to just leave, the door opened, and both Xander and Lillian walked out, looking surprised to see her.

***

Chapter 1

"Lillian," Xander said, with a slightly confused expression still on his face. "This is Sarah Shaw. She's Jayden's new secretary."

"Oh! It's *sooo* lovely to meet you," Lillian said, with an air of overdone friendliness. She offered her hand out to Mia for a handshake. "I'm Lillian Davis, a friend of Xander's. Are you enjoying working at Will Golden?"

"Yes, it's proving to be quite enjoyable," Mia replied.

"Glad to hear it. I hope everything works out well for you. Unfortunately, I'm late for a lunch, but I hope I'll run into you again soon, and we can get to know each other better." Lillian winked at Mia and started to walk away.

"It was nice to meet you!" Mia said with a wave.

As soon as Lillian was safely outside of the building, Xander grabbed Mia's wrist and pulled her back into his office, locking the door behind him. He kissed Mia passionately, running one hand through her long blonde hair and slowly caressing her curves with the other one.

"I know it's only been a few hours, but I've missed you," he said. "I can't get the last few days out of my mind."

But Mia wasn't as responsive as he had expected. She was kissing him back, but it felt like she was just going through the motions.

"What's going on with you?" he demanded. "Just a few hours ago we were fine. Tell me what's on your mind."

Mia shook her head. "It's nothing, really," she said.

Seeing Lillian there had really shaken her up. How was she supposed to be with Xander, and work at Will Golden for that matter, if she was keeping this secret?

"Are you jealous of Lillian?" he asked. "It's really nothing. I'll admit, she was the ex-girlfriend I had told you before, but you have absolutely nothing to worry about. We've been over for a long time. There's no chance of me getting back with her, ever. We were just talking about some financial and business related matters, so we could really finalize the breakup."

Although she was still feeling uncomfortable from her encounter with Lillian, Mia couldn't help but smile at how hard Xander was trying to convince her of his innocence. It was rather charming, how much he cared.

"It's okay, Xander, I believe you, really. I was just thinking about everything for a minute. We still have to deal with the whole Jayden situation, remember?"

"Ahh, don't worry about that now, gorgeous," Xander said. "Why don't I take you out to lunch? There's a new five-star restaurant on the Upper East Side that I'm dying to try out, and there's no one I'd rather dine with right now."

"As much as I would love that, Xander, I think I'll just grab a sandwich from the cafe across the street. I don't think we should be seen together in public yet, right? I mean, we don't want to cause a scandal or anything."

Xander sighed. "I guess you're right," he said. "But you'll have to make it up to me later." He gave her a quick little kiss on the lips and opened the door. "Enjoy your lunch, baby."

***

Chapter 2

Mia returned from lunch and went to set her coffee down on her desk outside Jayden's office. She was still feeling rattled by her encounter with Lillian earlier in the day. It was incredibly unexpected, and now she was worried about how she would handle her false identity problem.

How would she explain the situation to Xander? He was going to be so angry, for sure. And what if Lillian found out that she and Xander were together? Then Lillian would be mad at her too, and the last thing she needed were these two rich, powerful people on her bad side. And she still had to break up with Jayden… Just thinking about all of it was enough to give her a headache.

As she was walking to her desk, she passed a glass walled conference room. Xander was standing at the head of a table, giving a presentation of some sort to a group of men in black suits. This was when Mia found Xander the most appealing, when he was really in his element, charming his way into a deal with a group of soulless, power hungry Wall Streeters. She caught his eye as she was moving past the window, and he gave her an irresistibly sexy smirk. Mia instantly started to feel calmer. Things would work themselves out. She just had to give it some time.

When she reached Jayden's office, she was surprised to find a man sitting in the chair across from the desk. He was tall and dark haired, with an intense, almost cold face. He was wearing a gray suit that had to have cost him upwards of five thousand dollars.

"Hello," he said, standing up to shake Mia's hand. "My name is Robert Jackson. I am a Business Executive Developer for Greene Valley Holdings."

Mia didn't know much about the business side of Will Golden Corporation yet, but she recognized Greene Valley Holdings as the name of Xander's biggest business rival.

"What is this guy up to?" she thought. *"I can't imagine he's here for anything good."*

"If you're here to see my boss, Jayden Steele, he's out of town on business for the rest of the week, unfortunately," said Mia. "He's actually not even in the country right now, so it's going to be difficult to get a hold of him until he gets back."

"Actually," Robert said, coldly, "I'm here to talk to you, Mia."

Mia's blood ran cold, and her heart starting beating at triple its normal rate. How did this man know her real name?

"Oh, I know everything," Xander said with an evil grin. "I know you're Jayden Steele's girlfriend, not his secretary. And I also know that you're cheating on him with Alexander Will. Which is wonderfully convenient for me, because I need you to get both of them to do something. You see, there's this document, an agreement that Greene Valley Holdings has been trying to get Will Golden to sign for years. They never do, because it would result in significantly decreased profit margins, and probably the eventual downfall of the entire company. You're going to get both Alexander and Jayden to sign it."

"I... I can't do that," Mia stammered. "Why would I get them to sign a document that would bring down this entire company? I just can't."

"You can, and you will, because if you don't, I'll expose your whole scandalous life publicly. I don't think either Jayden or Xander would be particularly happy, if they learned that their precious Sarah Shaw was actually a detective named Mia Madison, would they? And on top of it, just in case you develop a conscience about the whole thing, I will pay you two hundred fifty thousand dollars to stay quiet."

Two hundred fifty thousand dollars!? That was triple what Lillian was paying her for this silly revenge plot. Mia had no idea what she would even do with that amount of money.

Just then, Xander walked into the office, a confused look on his face. Why was Robert here? He was always up to something conniving. Mia looked absolutely terrified.

"Robert," he said. "It's nice to see you again. What brings you in today?"

"Oh, I was looking for Jayden, but apparently he's abroad. So I was just having a little chat with... Sarah here. I'll be on my way out soon. It's nice to see you, Alexander."

Robert stood up to leave, and Mia exhaled deeply. He might have been the most terrifying man she had ever met, and she was extremely relieved to see him go, even though she had a sneaky feeling that he would be back, and he would continue to make her life a living hell until he got what he wanted.

Xander could see that whatever Robert had been saying had traumatized her, but he didn't want to stress her out more by talking about it right now. He decided that he would ask her later, when they were out of the office and in a more private situation.

"So, Sarah, *uhhh*, Jayden's clients are having an emergency meeting at that new five-star restaurant on the Upper East Side. I'm going to need you to come with me, since Jayden isn't here," he said with a wink. However, there were several people directly outside the office who could hear him. Mia had no choice but to go.

Once they were safely in the elevator, Mia grabbed Xander's hand and gave it a quick squeeze. "Well played, Xander," she whispered. She could not have been more grateful that he had walked into the office when he had, before Robert had gotten her to really do anything damaging.

***

Chapter 3

They sat quietly in the car on the way to the hotel. On top of everything she had been stressing about before, she now had to worry about the situation with Robert Jackson. How would she find her way out of this? She would have to come up with a plan sooner.

Xander was silent, and he seemed quite tense. Mia wondered how much of her conversation with Robert he had heard. He would be livid if he found out about any of it. *I should have just said no when Lillian asked me to take this job*, Mia thought. *Then I'd probably be at home right now, watching Netflix and waiting desperately for someone to email me with a new case.*

They arrived at the restaurant, which was on the first floor of one of the city's most respected hotels.

"Alexander Will, reservation for two, please," Xander said to the host.

They were lead through the dining room, which was elegantly decorated in rich burgundy colors, and featured a live string quartet playing softly in the corner. They were taken through a door at the back, which lead to an intimate private dining room. Mia was surprised at the lengths Xander had gone to get her alone.

"I hope this is sufficient, sir," said the host.

"It's exactly what I wanted," Xander said, handing him a hundred bill.

"A server will be back in a few minutes to take your orders."

They sat down at the table and began to peruse their menus.

"Why were you talking to Robert?" Xander asked angrily. "That man is always up to something. Was he flirting with you? Be honest with me."

"He wasn't flirting with me, I swear," Mia said, a tremor of nervousness in her voice. "He... he wanted to talk about this business deal with Jayden. It's not a big deal, really."

Xander looked at her, concern and worry in his eyes. He reached across the table and took her hand, making small circles on her palm with his thumb. Mia started to relax. "Please tell me what's going on, Sarah. I can tell that you're worrying about something, you're not looking your best. Whatever it is, I can handle it. I don't want you bottling all of this up."

"I really don't know much," Mia said. "It's something to do with a contract Robert wants Jayden to sign. He didn't give me too many details."

"Ahh, I see," Xander said. "You don't need to worry about this, Sarah. A few months ago, Robert came to Jayden, asking him to sign a deal that would bring the whole company down. He wanted to bribe him with a very large sum of money. Luckily, Jayden came to me afterwards, and told me what was going on. We decided he would keep meeting with Robert to placate him, so he doesn't go off and do anything aggressive or damaging. Jayden's been stalling on signing the deal for months. It's not going to happen. We have it under control."

Mia forced herself to smile. "Okay," she said. "I'm sorry I'm not myself right now. Robert's quite intimidating. He just really threw me for a loop, that's all."

"I know he's horrible to deal with, but just don't let him treat you like that, alright? He's not your problem, he's ours."

"I know. He really just wanted to talk to Jayden anyway, I don't know why he was even bothering me. Let's not worry about it. I want to enjoy our time together," Mia said, trying to divert the subject.

"Speaking of," Xander said with a flirtatious smile. "I booked us the luxury penthouse suite for tonight."

***

Chapter 4

Mia was in awe when she saw the suite Xander had booked. It had a bedroom, a living area with a fully equipped entertainment system, a bathroom with a spa area, and a kitchen with a fully stocked bar.

"Let's forget about work for the night," she said. "Tonight's going to be about us."

She grabbed Xander's hand and pulled him into the bedroom. She pushed him down on the bed and straddled him. She kissed him and started to work on undoing the buttons of his shirt, and he slowly pulled the zipper down on the back of her dress.

"I have a better idea," Xander said. "Why don't we take full advantage of this gorgeous spa bathroom. It's been a long day, I think we could both use a shower."

Mia stood up, taking her dress off completely in the process. "I would love to be with you in the shower," she uttered seductively.

Giggling like teenagers, they went into the bathroom and turned on the shower, which was a soothingly warm temperature. As the water started to drip down their backs, Xander ran his hands across Mia's breasts, down to her stomach, and finally between in her legs.

He slowly moved his fingers inside of her, making her moan with pleasure.

"Sarah," he whispered provocatively. "You are one beautiful masterpiece," he said, gazing at her with full desire lurking his face.

Mia, kissed him eagerly upon hearing his words. All of the stress of the day finally started to melt away. This was what she really needed --- an escape.

Voluntarily, she spreads her legs wider, so he can have an easier access. Xander's expression was darker now, thirsty, and longing. He continues to torture her body with his kisses and fingers, and when he was sure that she's ready, he whispered to her closely, and in a pleading manner.

"Baby, let me take you from behind."

Mia nodded, grinning and aching for him too. Xander flipped her around, and entered her from behind as steam started to fill the room. Slowly and eagerly, their bodies moved together in rhythm, picking up speed as they both tried to find and reach their ecstatic climaxes.

Arching her body, Mia gasped between his thrusts. She threw seductive glances to him as though, she was trying to motivate him to continue. She saw him, shutting his eyes and grunting in pleasure as he sinks in and out of her body.

Mia pushes her hips enthusiastically, moaning. Making love with Xander was the greatest thing that ever happened to her entire life.

Oh… Xander… please don't stop…

After a few more gratifying moves, Xander shifted her majestically. This time, he carried her and pinned her body on the wall. It didn't take long when Mia felt his enormous muscle once again. She was quite aware of its fullness and hardness, which made her feel more aroused.

"Baby…" Xander panted, then he claimed her mouth and Mia tasted his tongue. Until now, she couldn't believe that she can actually make him so hungry for her body.

When Mia opened her eyes again, she can see how Xander stares at her darkly, as if he lost his mind. She held him tighter as he pushed deeper. Then, Xander put her down and submerged her body in the lukewarm water, still filling her sex with his penis. He spreads her legs wider, and slams into her roughly.

"Xander! Oh, Damn!" Mia yelled appreciatively. She knew that both of them are getting closer and closer to their orgasms.

Xander didn't stop. He increases his speed, thrusting and filling Mia's yearning. "Let me see you come, Sarah," he ordered in a pleading tone.

As if it was the cue that she was waiting, Mia felt the numbing sensation of her legs. She willingly joined his rhythm for a few more seconds, panting, and calling out Xander's name in the process. Then... *there!* She releases her sweet climax abundantly, as Xander quickly joined her heaven.

"SARAH!" he growled at his final blow, then collapsing on top of her delightfully.

Fully satisfied, Xander stepped out of the shower and pulled on one of the hotel's famously fluffy bathrobes. He stopped to appreciate Mia's unclothed body, which was toned and wiry, as well as evenly tanned from their trip to the beach last week.

"You are so sexy, Sarah," he said, letting out a low whistle. "That was exactly what I needed after a long day at work. In fact, I think I'm going to call my secretary and ask her to cancel my appointments for tomorrow."

After Xander finished his phone call, he and Mia decided to relax in the hot tub together. They opened a bottle of red wine from the bar in the kitchen and ordered decadent chocolate desserts from room service. Everything was heavenly. Mia had never in her life experienced this level of luxury, and she wanted to soak it all up.

"You know what we should do?" Xander said, while licking a smear of whipped cream off his fingers. "We should have a cheesy movie marathon. We can start with *Sweet Home Alabama, Love Actually,* and *The Notebook.*"

"Xander Will enjoys *The Notebook?*" Mia said, astonished. "You're just full of endless surprises."

"Not to bring up my ex or anything, but Lillian had a thing for romantic movies. She was always making me watch them with her. After a while I realized I was starting to actually enjoy them. And given the look on your face, it clearly scores me some points in the romance department."

"I'll set up the TV if you open another bottle of wine?" Mia suggested.

"Sounds like a plan."

They spent the entire night cuddling on the couch, and Mia was shocked at how romantic Xander could actually be. It seemed as if his charming bad boy behavior was all just an act to make him seem stronger and less vulnerable in his role as a notable businessman. Mia felt a rush of affection for him.

He lets me see who he actually is, she thought. *Maybe it's not always perfect, but it's real.*

Mia and Xander woke up around two o'clock in the afternoon the next day. After watching four movies back to back, they had made love once more before falling asleep in the hotel's giant king sized bed. Xander turned to Mia as rays of sunshine were beaming through the window.

"Thank God I canceled all of my appointments for the day," he said.

"Thank God," Mia replied. She leaned over to kiss him, but was interrupted when she heard her phone buzzing on the bedside table. "I should probably look at this," she said with a groan.

The screen on her phone read an incoming call from Jayden Steele. "Hi, Jayden, can I call you back in half an hour?" she said, in a falsely cheery voice.

"Whatever you need, babe!" Jayden replied.

Mia hung up, and looked at Xander, who was shooting daggers at her with his eyes.

"I have to go," she said. "But don't worry, I'll break up with him today. We can't keep dragging this out."

***

Chapter 5

Mia called Jayden back once she was in the elevator.

"Do you want to go out to dinner tonight?" he asked.

Mia paused. She really didn't want to encourage him by going out to dinner. She should just break up with him now. But then again, he just got back from what had to be a long and stressful trip. It wasn't really fair to him to break it off now. She would do it at dinner, she thought. It would be hard, but she hated keeping this secret.

"Sure," she said. "Where are we going?"

"Oh, don't worry about that," Jayden said. "I'll pick you up."

"That's really not necessary," Mia said. "You can just text me the address and I'll meet you there."

"Are you sure?"

"Yeah, don't worry about it. See you tonight!" she said, forcing herself to sound positive, even though she was cringing inside at the thought of the inevitable breakup.

She walked into the restaurant Jayden had picked about six hours later, wearing an effortless flowy red dress. She had wanted to look nice, but she hadn't tried too hard since she didn't want to give Jayden the wrong impression. The restaurant he had chosen was very trendy and modern, almost minimal, the kind of place where your entree was more of a work of art than something actually edible.

She noticed Jayden sitting in a cozy table for two in the corner. He waved her over, with a huge smile on his face. Mia felt like her heart was about to beat out of her chest, she was so nervous. She didn't want to break up with him like this. She couldn't handle seeing him that upset right now. She would do it tomorrow, or something. Xander would just have to deal with it.

Although she had expected the date to go very poorly, the pair actually had a wonderful, lively conversation once they had ordered their food. Jayden told her all of his stories about his trip. Apparently there had been a baggage mix-up on the plane, and he'd ended up with a young girl's duffel bag instead of his own.

"So I opened the bag expecting to find my coat and my laptop, and instead I found a stuffed cat and a Gameboy… What are the odds that a six-year-old would have the same bag as me?" He laughed. Mia was surprised at how charming and funny he could be. She found that she was actually having a nice time. He wasn't Xander, of course, but it was still pleasant. He was a good guy.

They ordered a second bottle of wine, and continued chatting long after they had finished their food. Mia felt herself starting to get flushed and giggly, all the signs that she was tipsy and should probably stop drinking, but she poured herself another glass anyway. Maybe this would make her forget about Robert and his threats, and Xander, and Lillian, and how she was supposed to be breaking up with Jayden right now. So, she ended up flirting with him instead.

The restaurant slowly started to empty out, and Mia and Jayden were still there, drinking. The staff was starting to send them pointed looks, implying that they should leave soon.

"There's a really great bar a few blocks away," Jayden said. "Do you want to go?"

"You don't have to ask me twice," Mia said.

Xander sat in the back of his limo and watched Jayden and Mia exit the restaurant. The idea of them together made him nervous, almost physically ill. So, he had followed them there. Clearly, Mia had not broken up with him like she had said that she would. In fact, they were looking awfully cozy, with Jayden's arm around her waist.

Was Mia stumbling? She looked quite drunk. Silently, Xander got out of the car and began to follow them, making sure to keep a safe distance so he wouldn't be spotted.

Mia was sitting on the bar stool with her drink. She had switched from red wine to martinis at some point, although she couldn't really remember when. Although she was having a good time with Jayden, she still felt awful about the whole situation with Xander. She just kept thinking about her weekends away with him, spent in complete bliss.

Jayden came over to her, another drink in his hand. "You're looking a little sad, gorgeous," he said. "Anything on your mind?"

"No," she said, forcing a smile. "I was just a little zoned out."

"Well, why don't you come and dance with me?" he asked.

Soon, they were whirling around the dance floor. Mia was so drunk, she felt like the lights were spinning around her, and she clung to Jayden for balance. He started kissing her, and Mia knew she should resist, but she decided to let her worries melt away and just go with it instead.

After dancing for a while, they went back to sit at the bar for a bit, and Mia pulled out her phone. She had ten missed calls and texts from Xander! *What was going on? Maybe there was an emergency,* she thought. She opened one of the text messages, but it was so dark in the bar and she was so drunk that she couldn't actually read it. She decided to put her phone away and just deal with the problem later.

Jayden thought it was a little strange that Mia was being so wild tonight, but he was glad that she was having a good time. "Sarah, do you want to get out of here?" he asked hopefully. "My place is just a few blocks uptown."

Mia was too drunk to do anything other than nod, but she knew she would regret her decision in the morning.

***

Chapter 6

Xander decided he couldn't stand to watch this anymore. He had to do something before Mia got any more intoxicated and actually slept with Jayden.

"Hey!" he yelled. "Jayden! What are you guys doing here?"

"We were just out on a date," Jayden said. "What are you doing here"

"Um.. I was just waiting for a friend, and I saw you guys. I think I should take Sarah here home. She looks like she's had a little too much."

"No, that's okay, I got it," Jayden said, looking confused. "She's my girlfriend, after all. You don't need to worry about it."

"You know, Jayden, I trust you, but I would feel better if I at least came with you and make sure she got home in one piece. After all, you've been drinking too."

"Alright, whatever you say, boss," Jayden said, completely bewildered by Xander's possessive behavior.

They decided to use Jayden's car to take Mia home. She was so drunk, she couldn't even give them an address, so Xander called the head of the HR department at Will Golden to get it.

Mia was passing in and out of consciousness the entire car ride home. At some point she started crying.

"What's wrong, hon?" Jayden asked, concerned. Xander glared at him in the rearview mirror.

"I.. I *dunno*. Everything.. everything's spinning." Mia said, bawling. "I *wanna* go *hoommmeee*."

"We're almost there!" Xander said, trying to calm her down. "We'll get you home and tucked in bed with a glass of water, okay? Just try and keep it together for a few more minutes."

By the time they finally found Mia's place, she was totally passed out in the backseat. Xander and Jayden had to carry her up three flights of stairs to her apartment.

"I'm so sorry about this," Jayden said. "She's not normally like this, she's normally very reasonable at parties. I don't know why she got so crazy tonight. I should have stopped her."

"I'm just doing this for the company's reputation," Xander said, coldly. "And for yours. She's your secretary, after all. And our employees can't be seen in public behaving like this. We have an image to maintain. It's for both of your own good, I promise."

***

Chapter 7

Xander had to pick the lock on Mia's door, because she was too intoxicated to find her key. Jayden then carried her to her room and started helping her clean up. He helped her wash her face and got her a glass of water, and then slowly started undressing her so she could take a shower.

Xander felt extremely frustrated. He wanted to stop Jayden, tell him that, she was his girl, and that she didn't care about him. But he had promised Mia that she could be the one to tell him, so he kept his mouth shut.

But still, he watched Jayden, who was taking care of her so gently, and he wished he was the one doing it to her. He kept his eyes on them to make sure Jayden didn't take advantage of Mia, but started looking for a set of tools to fix Mia's lock, which he had broken. He finally found a set under the sink.

As he was fixing the door, Jayden came out of Mia's room.

"I think she's going to be all right," he said. "She just needs to sleep it off. I think I've learned my lesson about taking her to the bar, poor thing."

"Thanks for taking care of her, Jayden," Xander said reluctantly. "I'm not too sure what's going on with her, I don't think she's always like that. I haven't had a chance to tell you this yet, but Robert Jackson stopped by your office while you were gone. I was passing by and I happened to notice him talking to Sarah. I don't know what exactly he said, but she was white as a sheet. He clearly was making her nervous."

"Do you think this has something to do with that horrible deal he wants me to sign?" Jayden asked. "I've been trying to put him off as long as possible, but I think he's starting to catch on to the fact that I'm not actually planning on signing it."

"Sarah said that it had something to do with that, but she wouldn't give me any details," Xander said. "I think he might be threatening her or blackmailing her in some way. I don't know if he knows about the nature of your relationship with her, but I think he believes that she can influence you to sign it."

"I'll have to ask her about it myself when she's feeling better," Jayden said. "If she tells me what's really going on, we can fix this. She shouldn't have to deal with it by herself."

"I agree," Xander said. "Just please watch out for her, okay? She seemed really scared. I don't want her to get in over her head with this."

"I will. But I think for now, we should probably both go home and get some sleep. It's been a long night."

"I'll be right behind you, I just have to finish putting in this last screw, and then I'll be right down. Do you want me to drive you home? I know you've been drinking, and I want you to stay safe."

"Sure, that will be fine" Jayden said.

They took his car and Xander dropped Jayden off. After safely parking Jayden's car in the garage of his building, he called his limo back and circled around to Mia's apartment again.

***

Chapter 8

When Xander had been fixing the lock on Mia's door, he found a spare key hanging on the wall next to the door inside the apartment. He had sneakily taken it without Jayden noticing, so he could get back into the apartment later. He snuck up the staircase of Mia's walk-up and made his way inside as quietly as he possibly could. He wanted to stay the night with her and make sure she was okay. She'd been acting strangely all day, and he was very worried about her.

He opened the door to Mia's bedroom to find her in a very deep sleep. She had washed her hair and was wearing an old, oversized UCLA sweatshirt. He gently lay down next to her on the bed and pulled her into his arms. She was sleeping very fretfully, and he tried to soothe her as much as he could, even though she was sleeping.

"I'm sorry!" Mia said, vehemently. Xander jumped, as he hadn't expected the noise. He then realized that she was talking in her sleep. "I didn't mean it!" she kept saying. "I didn't mean to do it! I'm sorry!"

"Shh..." Xander said softly. "It's okay, Sarah. It's going to be alright," he added worriedly. However, she was so deep into her dream that she didn't hear him.

He was still extremely worried about her. What had Robert said to her yesterday that was making her so scared and tense? But he realized that he was no longer angry about her date with Jayden. Clearly, she was under a lot of stress, it was understandable that she didn't want to break up with him right now. Everything would work itself out later, he hoped.

Mia work up with a start. She was instantly confused. Why was Xander here, in her apartment!? What had happened last night?

She remembered being with Jayden, and having a few drinks at a bar, but she couldn't really remember anything that had happened after that. How had she gotten home, and when had Xander shown up? Her head was throbbing. She had to find out what was going on.

"Xander?" she said, gently tapping him awake. "What's.. what's going on?"

"Oh, Sarah, you're awake!" Xander said brightly. "How are you feeling? You had quite the night last night!"

Mia groaned. "I don't really remember what happened at all," she said.

"You went out with Jayden last night, remember? I found you at a bar, completely out of control. You were all over him, Sarah! What happened to our plan of breaking things off? You've almost made the situation worse now."

"I know," she said, tears starting to fill her eyes. "But I saw how happy he was to see me, and I just couldn't do it! It didn't feel right. I got cold feet. I'm so sorry, Xander. I know this isn't fair to you, or to Jayden."

"It's okay," Xander said, calming down now. "We can always deal with it later. Right now, I just want to make sure you're okay. I doubled back here after Jayden left last night, because I was so worried about you."

"Speaking of, how did you get my address?" Mia asked. She was starting to get concerned about the fact that Xander and Jayden had both been in her apartment all night. What if they had found evidence of her secret identity, or her deal with Lillian?

"Oh, I called one of the HR people at Will Golden," Xander said casually. "I figured they would have it. I hope you don't mind."

"No, not at all," Mia said. For now, her cover seemed safely intact. She looked around the apartment. Everything seemed to be in order. None of her mail, or her computer for her detective business, had been disrupted.

"Hey," Xander said, tenderly grabbing her hand. "I have an idea. What if we go out of town again? I think you really need to rest after all of the excitement and stress you've had over the past few days. We can go back to Southampton, do it right this time."

"Are you sure we can take that much time off of work? We already skipped out early the other day."

"I'm the boss," Xander said with an arrogant grin. "I can do whatever I want. And Jayden's not going to expect you to be up to doing secretarial work, after the night that you had."

"Well, I guess you'd better call your limo, then," Mia said, with a wink.

Xander and Mia spent the day on Xander's private island again, relaxing on the beach with some sandwiches they had picked up on their way out of the city. They were really enjoying each other's company, joking around and making each other laugh. But there was one problem. Jayden kept texting Mia, trying to check up on her.

After the fifth text message, Xander grabbed her phone away, tackling her in the process. "That's it, I'm taking this!" he said, as they playfully rolled around in the sand. "You're all mine today."

"No, Xander, he's just trying to be nice," Mia said. "I'm not going to answer him or anything."

"No, see, this is payback for not breaking up with him," Xander said sarcastically. "No breakup, no phone." He winked at her, but he still took her phone and went into the house, hiding it in his locked briefcase.

"Now, where were we?" he said when he came back out, finding Mia lying on the beach, eyes closed, wearing a bikini that showed off her perfectly toned stomach. He laid down next to her, and leaned over, kissing her deeply. He then pulled her on top of him, and slowly reached up to untie the strings of her bikini.

"Are you sure it's a good idea to do this outside?" Mia said to him. "We're sure there's no one else on this island, right?

"It's just you and me, babe," he replied. "My family bought this island a few generations ago, and I'm pretty sure I'm the only one that still comes here. We're totally safe."

They continue to make out, and Mia started grinding her hips against his. She could feel him starting to develop an erection, and reached down to slowly remove his swim trunks. She took off her bikini bottoms and moved him inside of her, slowly and deliberately.

"Damn it, Sarah," Xander said in a low moan. "That feels incredible."

She slowly started to ride him, picking up speed as she went along. Although she had been worried, Mia loved the adrenaline rush of having sex outside, where anyone could have seen them. They climaxed at the same time, and she slowly rolled off of him, lying next to him in the sand again. She leaned over and kissed his neck sensually.

After a few minutes, Mia fell asleep. Xander carried her into the beach house and set her down on the bed in the master bedroom, and then joined her for a nap.

After a few hours, Xander was awakened by the pinging noise of Mia's phone receiving a text message. Thinking that it was Jayden, sending another one of his "caring" texts, he grabbed Mia's phone out of his briefcase.

After looking at the number for a minute, he realized that it was Lillian texting Mia! *How do they know each other?*

Hey love, how's our little plan going? Looked like you were doing a great job when I saw you the other day! Keep it up!

Xander was instantly confused, and terrified. *What plan!?* Panicked, he started looking through the rest of her phone. He found out that her name was Mia, not Sarah, and that she was a private detective. It seemed that Lillian had hired her to look into Xander's suspicious activity when they were still dating, and then when they broke up, she hired her to get revenge on him by seducing and then dumping him. Although, she hadn't dumped him yet, which meant that clearly something was going wrong, because she'd had plenty of opportunity to.

Xander was absolutely furious. Why would these women do this to him!? Sure, he'd cheated a few times, and he knew it was wrong, but he didn't think he deserved this sort of elaborate punishment. Shaking, he put Mia's phone back in her bag, and tapped her on the shoulder to wake her up. It was time to go home.

Xander was extremely quiet on the ride home, to the point where Mia was starting to get worried. She thought they'd had a wonderful little afternoon getaway. After all, what was more romantic than sex on the beach?

"Xander, what's wrong?" she asked. "You're awfully quiet."

Xander's face was stone cold. "Oh, I don't know, *Mia*," he said acidly. "Maybe, it has something to with the fact that you've been plotting revenge against me with my ex-girlfriend the entire time I've known you?"

Mia's heart practically stopped beating. *He knew.*

"H-how... when?" she stuttered.

"I saw a text from Lillian on your phone. I was obviously confused by that, so I did a little digging. Did you really think you were just going to be able to hide this from me forever? Even if you didn't go through with Lillian's plan, I still was going to find out about it eventually. Was this whole thing a lie, Mia?"

"No!" she yelled, in tears. "It may have started off as something I was just doing for Lillian, but it's certainly much more than that now. I was going to tell Lillian the plan was off and give her money back. I just haven't had the time yet, what with everything that's been going on at work."

"I don't really want to hear your excuses right now," Xander said. "You know what, actually, I'm just going to have the driver drop you off here. You can find your own way home."

***

Chapter 9

Mia was still standing at a bus stop in outer Brooklyn, crying, when Jayden pulled up in his car.

"Sarah? What are you doing here?" he said, bewildered.

Mia was crying so hard, she couldn't get the words out. "It's.. it's a long story."

"Well, why don't you get in the car, and I'll take you home, okay? What are you even doing out here, anyway?"

"I just had something I had to do… I really don't want to talk about it right now."

"You know what?" Jayden asked. "Why don't I take you to see the fireworks on Coney Island tonight."

"Okay," Mia said, too exhausted to protest.

Later that evening, Mia and Jayden were sitting on the beach, watching the fireworks and eating cotton candy. Jayden had his arm around her, and even though Mia felt extremely guilty for everything that had happened, she was actually having a pleasant time. But then, Jayden leaned in to kiss her, and she decided she couldn't lie to him anymore either.

"Jayden, I can't do this. I have something to tell you. Please don't hate me. I never meant to do you any harm."

She told him the entire story, from Lillian hiring her to investigate Xander, to Robert Jackson blackmailing her, and everything that had happened in between. Although Jayden seemed a little put off at first, he was eventually sympathetic to her story.

"I'm not coming back to work," Mia said. "I just got in way over my head. I never meant to hurt anyone, I swear. I was never going to go through with the revenge plan. And I do like you a lot, Jayden. You're a really great guy. I'm just sorry we met under these circumstances."

"I understand, Mia. I'm really sorry you got caught in the middle of all of our drama. I'm disappointed, but I wish you luck with everything. "

"I hope all this stuff with Robert Jackson works out. He's one scary guy."

"He sure is. Why don't I drive you home now?"

Mia cried in the car the entire way home. She was so upset about the way everything had happened. She truly loved Xander, and she had hurt him terribly. Even though he wasn't always the best guy, she knew she wanted to be with him, and now that would never happen.

She sat down to send an email to Lillian. She informed her that she would be quitting the job and refunding her money, and that Xander had found out the truth about everything. She left out the part about her and Xander actually falling in love. She wanted to keep that between them.

She pressed send and then went to bed for the night. She cried herself to sleep, and slept fretfully until she was awakened around one in the morning by a loud, forceful knock at the door. She went to go answer it, and found an unidentified man standing there. Before she could ask him who he was, he grabbed her, covered her mouth, and put a black bag over her head. She felt like she was drowning. She couldn't breathe at all. She tried to scream but didn't have any air in her lungs. So, eventually she passed out into her kidnapper's arms.

Mia woke up in a vacant and run-down warehouse, tied to a chair. The man who had taken her was there, keeping an eye on her.

"Who are you?" she screamed. "What is this!? Why did you take me!?" She started to cry again.

She didn't think she had ever cried so much in her life, and wondered if her body would ever run out of tears.

"I work for Robert Jackson," the man said. "He will be here any minute. He wants to speak with you."

Robert entered the warehouse a few minutes later, wearing his usual expensive suit and tie. Mia wondered what time it was . Was it still the middle of the night? Or had the day started? Where were Xander and Jayden, were they at work right now? They were probably her only hope of getting out of here alive. Although, given the information they had found out last night, she wasn't sure either of them would actually want to save her.

"I'm sending a picture of you to Xander." Robert said, pulling out his camera phone. "If he doesn't sign the contract in the next four hours, you will die. Simple as that."

"Xander won't care," Mia said. "We had a huge fight last night. He wants me out of his life completely."

"I don't believe that," Robert said. "You have a hold over him, and Jayden too. This will work. I'm sure they will be banging down the doors of this place as fast as they can get their limos over here."

Mia shook her head. She was sure she was going to die.

"You weren't there last night!" she screamed. "You don't know how angry he was!" And with that, she closed her eyes and waited to die.

***

After waiting for over three hours, Mia decided that there had to be something she could do to escape. She started messing with the knots in the rope that was holding her to the chair. Luckily, she realized that one of the threads was loose. She kept picking at it when her captors weren't looking at her. She was pretty sure if she could just undo the knot, she could run faster than Robert and his guard. After all, she'd been an athlete in college, and neither of them looked like they were in great shape.

After half an hour of undoing the knot, it finally came loose. Mia ran as fast as she possibly could, heading for the door to the warehouse. Robert and his guard started shouting. Just as she opened the door, she felt a searing pain in her right shoulder blade. Robert had shot her. She managed to make it out of the warehouse and into an alley a few blocks away, but at that point she was bleeding so heavily she couldn't go on. She had to hide. Robert would be coming for her.

She turned around at the sound of sirens passing. Xander's limo stopped behind three police cars. He had come to her rescue! He saw him jumped out of the car and rushed towards her direction.

"Mia!" Xander said as he picked her up in his arms. He looked agitated and apprehensive. Mia was starting to feel woozy due to the amount of blood she was losing. She tried to reach and hold him, but she passed out, once again just before he could utter a word.

***

Epilogue

A few days later, Mia woke up in the hospital. Her best friend Lily was there with Xander, looking over her bedside.

"What happened?" Mia groaned. "How long has it been?"

"You escaped Robert and his guard, but you were shot," Xander said.

"Oh. Oh, that's right. God, what an insane week," Mia said, tearfully. She was actually referring about her whole affair with Xander, and not this particular incident. Then, she turned to both of them with teary eyes.

"I'm really glad to see you both here," she stated.

Lily leaned over and gave Mia's hand a quick squeeze.

"I'm glad you're alright," she said, thoughtfully. "I'm going to give you two some privacy," she added and walked out of the room.

Mia looked up at Xander, unable to comprehend what's on his mind. So much had happened between them at this point that she didn't know where to start.

"I'm sorry," they both said at the same time, and then both laughed.

"Mia, will you give me another chance?" Xander said, holding her hands. "I was too quick to judge you before. I want to hear your side of the story. Because the truth is, I'm in love with you, and nothing is going to change that for me."

"Xander," Mia said, sobbing in an instant. "I should have told you the whole truth earlier. I was never going to go through with

Lillian's revenge plan, because once I actually met you, I realized that I was falling in love with you too."

"I know," Xander whispered. "I can feel how you're sincerely in love with me every time we were together. I was so dumb to actually doubt you, baby," he admitted.

Mia finally burst into tears. "You have no idea how you made me glad for this," she said. From now on, you don't have to worry about Jayden. And I already broke up with him that night. I told him everything, and there are no hard feelings."

"Yeah, I heard about that," he replied, a trace of triumph was evident on his face. He leaned over and gave her a gentle kiss on the lips. "Well, I guess now we can start over together," he added happily.

"I-I think so," Mia answered, kissing him back.

"Oh, God! I swear I love you, Mia," he uttered, holding her completely.

"I love you, too, Mr. Will," she said, as Xander wiped the tears in her eyes.

THE END

Here are other titles from Dark Mocco that you might enjoy!

Triple The Pleasure

Fanged

Satisfied

Dragon's Desire

The Fallen Revenge

Claimed By Dragons

Awakening The Dragon

Double Trouble

Billionaire's Secrets

Billionaires Pleasure

Chosen By Vampires

Mated By Shifters

Shifters Desire

www.ingramcontent.com/pod-product-compliance
Lightning Source LLC
Chambersburg PA
CBHW021118250825
31623CB00016B/43